You can't go home again.

They had tried to convince him not to go back, but he had felt that he had to see the house one more time and make sure that no one had returned to it. Not that he believed otherwise—but believing was not the same as seeing, touching, and smelling. And in fact, the Pitlaks' smell had put a stop to all of his fantasies since the war's end. He now knew deep down that he was alone in the world. . . .

OTHER PUFFIN BOOKS YOU MAY ENJOY

The Lady
with the Hat

Uri Orlev

Translated from the Hebrew by Hillel Halkin

PUFFIN BOOKS

PUFFIN BOOKS

Published by the Penguin Group

Penguin Putnam Inc., 375 Hudson Street, New York, New York 10014, U.S.A.

Penguin Books Ltd, 27 Wrights Lane, London W8 5TZ, England

Penguin Books Australia Ltd, Ringwood, Victoria, Australia

Penguin Books Canada Ltd, 10 Alcorn Avenue, Toronto, Ontario, Canada M4V 3B2

Penguin Books (N.Z.) Ltd, 182-190 Wairau Road, Auckland 10, New Zealand

Penguin Books Ltd, Registered Offices: Harmondsworth, Middlesex, England

First published in Israel by Keter Publishing House, 1990
First published in the United States of America by Houghton Mifflin Company,
1995
Reprinted by arrangement with Houghton Mifflin Company
Published in Puffin Books, 1997

1 3 5 7 9 10 8 6 4 2

LIBRARY OF CONGRESS CATALOGING-IN-PUBLICATION DATA
Orlev, Uri.
The lady with the hat / Uri Orlev : translated from the Hebrew by Hillel Halkin.
p. cm.
Summary: In 1947, seventeen-year-old Yulek, the only member of his immediate
family to survive the German concentration camps, joins a group of
young Jews preparing to live on a kibbutz in Israel, unaware
that his aunt in London is looking for him.
ISBN 0-14-038571-1 (pbk.)
[1. Holocaust survivors—Fiction. 2. Jews—Fiction.
3. Kibbutzim—Fiction.] I. Halkin, Hillel. II. Title.
PZ7.O633Lad 1997 97-15203 CIP AC

Printed in the United States of America

Contents

1.
Going Home

Yulek slipped off the crowded train and leaped onto the platform. No one else got off. He stood with his back to the town hall, waiting for the train to pull out and disappear around the bend near the forest. Not until he was sure that he was alone did he turn to look at his birthplace.

The town was the same as when he last had seen it from the station on the day they were loaded into boxcars and shipped to a concentration camp. Nothing had changed. The houses looked a bit smaller, perhaps because he was now seventeen, but the trees, which had gone on growing, were as big as ever. Here and there something was missing, a house that had been burned or destroyed; but after the shock of ruined Warsaw, he breathed a sigh of relief. Was it too much to hope for? Could someone from his family have survived and returned? Two years had passed since the end of the war, but only now, before leaving for Palestine, had he decided to come back one last time. And only now did he have money for the trip. Thanks to Robert, of course.

He had grown up in a two-story house with two wings, a large courtyard, and a stable used as a storeroom after the death of his grandfather, who had kept two horses and a wagon in it. The house belonged to

Yulek's paternal grandparents. After their marriage, Yulek's parents had lived on the top floor.

Yulek had learned that clock time was not real time. When selections for the gas chambers were made in the concentration camps that he and his father had been in, a month or even a year might seem to elapse between morning and evening. Those years during the war now felt as if they had been lived on another planet that had nothing to do with his real life. *Real* life had been here with his parents, and now he had returned to where it left off.

Yulek followed the half-paved, potholed road into town. It was early morning and the streets were empty. A few dogs began to bark. He turned the corner by the church and started up the main street. The shops were closed. He knew every one of them — the bakery, the grocery store, the pharmacy — but something was wrong. Of course! The Yiddish signs were gone. He should have known. Although he had seen the signs being taken down when the German army arrived, he now realized that he had gone on hoping to find the town looking exactly like his childhood memories.

He walked slowly. He wasn't in any hurry. And perhaps he wanted to postpone the disappointment, the moment in which the childish hope that had flared and gone on flickering since boarding the train in Rome would go out for good.

"Yulek?"

He gave a start, then halted and looked around. It was little Bashka, the baker's daughter.

"Hey, wait!" She shut the window and appeared a

second later in the doorway, wrapped in a large shawl. Before him stood not the girl he remembered but a buxom teenager. Only her expression was unchanged — the same closely set blue eyes staring out from a round face in which stupidity vied with good nature.

"Yulek, don't go to your home! It's a good thing I saw you. You look the same. You're just . . . older."

Her laugh, still halfway between a girlish giggle and a horsy whinny, was the same too. Stifling it with a hand, she whispered, "I'll catch hell if I wake up my mother." Then she added, "He's been waiting a long time for you with that shotgun of his. Not that I think he still expects any of you to turn up."

"Who are you talking about?"

"You don't know who's living in your house? What a dope I am! Of course you don't. It's Pitlak the forester."

Yulek smiled. Bashka had whispered "Pitlak the forester" in the same tone of voice they had used as frightened children when they were about to run from him.

"Does he still work in the forest?"

"No. He's the local Communist party boss. He's worse than ever. He walks around all the time with a gun and says it's to protect against wolves. And he has a new wife. Did you know that a German soldier walked off with his old one?"

She laughed again, then covered her mouth with an anxious glance at the windows.

"What a dope I am! How could you have known? He has a new wife, and they have four kids, and there's a fifth on the way." She wiped the mysterious grin off her face.

"I didn't come for the house," Yulek said, then added hesitantly, "Maybe I'll sell it." He wished Robert were with him. Robert would make a big scene and come away with his pockets full of money. He should at least try to get enough for the house to reimburse Robert for the train trip. Bashka was still chattering away. Again he heard the name Pitlak.

"He told my father long ago that he would kill any Jew who asked for the house back. He'd do it too. He killed his way through the war."

She grinned again. "I'm glad I saw you. I knew who you were right away." When she smiled without whinnying or gaping, she didn't seem so stupid. She looked so much like a friendly dog that as a boy he had had to restrain himself from petting her.

"Am I the only one who's come back?" he asked.

"Two of the tailor's children did too. And the cattle dealer's son. They were made to leave. And the grocer came with an army officer. The officer said he should be paid for his house and his store. You should have heard the screams. My father thought there would be blood, but it didn't come to that. This is no place for Jews anymore."

"The houses were theirs, Bashka. You know that."

"My father says that the house goes with the land. And the land is Polish, not Jewish. This is no place for Jews."

"I'm going to Palestine," Yulek said. "I'm going to be a farmer there."

"A farmer? You're too smart for that. Why don't you be a lawyer or a doctor or something?"

"Palestine needs farmers."

"My father says that because of the Communists there soon won't be any farmers left in Poland."

"What else does he say?"

Bashka looked around her and whispered, "He hates the Communists. The Germans weren't any better, but at least they got rid of the Jews. The Communists are on the Jews' side. My father says that the Jews are everywhere, even in the army and the government. They came back from Russia and from Germany and took over. They and the Communists help each other. My father says it's always been like that."

"I want to see our house. Do you really think it's dangerous?"

"No . . . I mean . . . well, he won't kill you. Too much time has gone by, and besides, he's party boss. There was this Englishwoman here . . ." Bashka giggled.

"What's so funny?"

"You should have seen the hat she had on! She belonged to your family, and she wanted to see the house, and —" Bashka caught herself.

"An Englishwoman?"

"My father told me not to tell. She came with an officer in a limousine from Warsaw. She was someone important, a real lady. She wanted to know if any of your family had come back, and she asked to see the house. So they took her to that dump that the Piotr-kowskis live in, the house that once belonged to the Zylbermans. They told her that during the war you had sold your big house and bought that one. Pitlak said that he saw your family killed with his own eyes. That

-5-

you Jews were all taken to the forest and shot there. He even took her to see the graves of some Jews, the ones found hiding in Koczik's hayloft. You were gone by the time that happened. She gave them money for a proper tombstone."

"Did they use it for that?"

"No. Pitlak pocketed the money. He gave some of it to the priest. My father says we shouldn't put the names of Jews on tombstones, because some of them might still be alive. Wait. I'll ask him if you can come in."

She vanished into the house without waiting for an answer.

Yulek wondered. An Englishwoman?

He vaguely remembered his aunt Malka. He could picture her leaning over him and handing him a large, wooden toy car. He could still feel how happy it had made him. Perhaps it had been for his birthday. How old would he have been? Maybe three. Or else four. He remembered her tall grace and even the quick way she crossed the courtyard with a bucket of water or with feed for the hens. Perhaps this was because, unlike the other women in the household, she didn't slip wordlessly away when his grandfather appeared. She had acted more like an uncle than an aunt. And then she had vanished.

A few years went by, and one day he found a book by his mother's bed with an intriguing illustration on the cover. He recalled it perfectly: it was of a diver walking on the bottom of the sea. He began turning the pages in the hope of finding more pictures and came across an envelope with a strange stamp. He knew that the man on it was the king of England and decided to ask if he could have it, because it wasn't in his collection. As he was fingering the envelope, he felt something stiff inside. It was a letter, inside which was a photograph of a bride and groom. The groom looked elegant in his top hat, and the bride seemed familiar. Yet no matter how hard he tried, he couldn't place her. Maybe she was a princess.

He ran with the envelope to the kitchen, calling out, "Mama! Mama!"

"What is it?" asked his mother.

She came toward him and turned pale when she saw what he had. She shut the door.

"Did Grandfather see you with that?"

"No, Mama." He was frightened by her fright.

"Did anyone see this letter? Your sisters?"

"They're not home." His two sisters had gone off with his father to visit Uncle Yisro'el in the city, and Yulek was surprised that his mother hadn't remembered.

"You're right," she said sheepishly. "I forgot. Did you look inside the envelope?"

"Yes," Yulek said. "There's a picture of a bride and groom. Are they a prince and a princess? The bride . . ." All at once he remembered. "It's Aunt Malka!" he cried happily.

"Hush!" said his mother. "You know perfectly well that Aunt Malka died long ago."

He did know that. She had gone abroad and died of some illness. His parents had told his sisters, who had then told him.

"Did she get married before that?" he asked.

"Yes. But it's a secret. No one must know. This is an old letter. I was just using it as a bookmark, do you understand?"

"Did she marry a Christian?"

"I'll tell you everything when you're older. Right now you have to promise not to mention it to anyone. Not to Grandfather, not to Grandmother, not even to your sisters."

"Not even to Papa?"

"Not even to Papa."

"But I want the stamp."

"You can have it if you don't tell. If you do, I'll take it back."

"All right, Mama."

So it was his aunt Malka who had come looking for them! Yulek thought. The memory of her made the house come alive in his mind. Pitlak or no Pitlak, he had to see it.

Bashka had not returned. Yulek glanced up and saw a curtain quickly close on a window. They had been observing him.

He decided not to wait. Bashka wouldn't be taking so long if they wanted to invite him in. Pitlak. Robert would laugh at him if he didn't at least give it a try.

Yulek started up the street with a firm stride. None of the few people he passed showed any sign of recognition. He too could not remember all their names, although their faces looked familiar. He didn't stop to say hello.

The house looked just as he had imagined it. For a minute he was able to pretend that there never had been any war and that he was simply coming home from the grocery store. The illusion was so perfect that he even heard the front door creak as it always did when his mother came to help him with the shopping basket, a big smile on her face.

But although the door had creaked all right, it was Pitlak with a double-barreled shotgun. Bashka's father must have sent one of the boys to run ahead and tell him. He was expecting Yulek, no doubt about it.

"Good morning, Pan Pitlak," Yulek said, trying to sound calm and confident.

"Good morning, Yulek. Where's your father?" Pitlak's face had a threatening look.

"He died in the camps."

"Look, Yulek," Pitlak said. "I'm not a forester anymore. I'm party boss." His voice brimmed with pride. "Poland belongs to the Poles now, do you get it? And this house is ours. But if you'll sign a document that I've prepared, I'll give you some money for the road."

"All right," said Yulek. There was a lump in his throat.

Pitlak invited him in. Yulek's heart pounded. The furniture had been moved around and the kitchen had been changed. There were a few new things, including the stove. Yulek thought of asking to go upstairs but decided against it. For a moment, although Pitlak never took his probing eyes off him, Yulek forgot that the ex-forester was there.

"There was a carton of Jewish books that I gave to some rabbi," Pitlak said, trying to guess Yulek's thoughts.

Yulek nodded. Pictures of the Catholic saints hung on the walls, and there was a different smell. Only now did he realize that this smell was the reason for the shock of strangeness he had felt upon entering.

Pitlak offered him a seat at the kitchen table. Yulek wavered, circled the table, and sat down in his father's old chair at the head of it. Pitlak nodded as if in acknowledgment and opened a drawer in which Yulek's father had kept his accounts. He reached for a brown cardboard folder, pulled out several sheets of paper, and gave them to Yulek to read and sign.

"The price is already stated. It's what the party decided on."

"Who's the party?" asked Yulek innocently

"I am," answered Pitlak, a roll of thunder in his voice.

Yulek no longer regretted Robert's absence. His sole desire was to get away as fast as possible. His eyes filled with tears at the sight of this house, which had ceased being his, though the ghosts of his family still hovered around the table. He did not bother to read what he signed. Pitlak returned the folder and drew a wad of bills from his pocket. Did all party bosses walk around with their pockets full of money?

Yulek heard whispers in the hallway, where, he now noticed, Pitlak's family was crowding together, curiously peeking at him through a curtain. A little boy asked loudly, "Is that the Jew? Is it?"

A woman tried shushing him.

"Is that the Jew who came to take our house away?" the boy asked anxiously. He squealed angrily as he was dragged away.

Yulek asked, "And no one else from my family has been here, Pan Pitlak?"

"No. I guess that means you're the sole landlord. Or were." He laughed. "You can take the money with a good conscience. It's all yours."

"No one, Pan Pitlak?" repeated Yulek stubbornly.

The man looked at him sharply and said, "No. I'm sorry to say it, but the Germans did us a big favor. You know what I mean. And now it's time you were on your way."

Yulek rose and left without a word, taking a roundabout route to the station to avoid Bashka's house and to see for the last time the narrow streets that he and his boyhood friends had played in. Pitlak's son had been one of these friends, a little hoodlum like his father.

Nothing was as he had thought it would be when he had tried imagining postwar Poland on the train ride through Germany. Here and there he had met Poles, generally enthusiastic and young, who honestly believed that they were building a new and happier society. But everywhere he had found hatred for the Russians, who had brought communism to Poland, and the old Polish hatred for the Jews. Young Jews who had come from Poland to Yulek's Zionist training camp in Italy had told about anti-Jewish pogroms committed not by the Nazis but by Poles. They had tried to persuade him not to go back, but he had felt that he had to see the house one more time and make sure that no one had returned to it. Not that he believed otherwise, but believing was not the same as seeing, touching, and smelling. And in fact, the Pitlaks' smell had put a stop to all his fantasies since the war's end. He now knew deep down that he was alone in the world.

Yulek thought of the Englishwoman. She seemed like a far-off beacon glimmering in the great darkness of his solitude.

There was a long wait for the train, and it was full when it arrived. Yulek was lucky to find a place to squeeze into between the baskets of eggs, vegetables, and cackling hens that were being taken to market by fat peasant women wearing brightly colored skirts and aprons and flowery kerchiefs.

He pulled his cap down over his eyes and feigned sleep while thinking of the cloudy future that awaited him in a distant land — the same Land of Israel of which there had been a map on his grandfather's blue and white collection box, filled with coins meant to help buy the land acre by acre until it was reclaimed. The Jews, Yulek thought, would do a better job of rebuilding their country than the Poles would. They would not hate anyone, and all who had been persecuted for two thousand years would come to live there. First, though, it was necessary to end English control of the country.

It was odd that the same English troops who had liberated Yulek from the concentration camp were now the enemy.

He remembered that day well. It was a sunny one in

spring, and his father had not lived to see it. How he had hoped that they would both be alive when it came.

At first his father had been the stronger of the two, supporting Yulek and keeping him going. Gradually, though, he weakened. Hunger and the viciousness of the German camp guards got the better of him, and it became Yulek who had to sustain *him*. The night after they were transferred to a camp in Germany, just two weeks before the arrival of the English, his father died. Yulek dragged the corpse to the morning roll call so that no one would be listed as missing. That was how they had parted.

Sometimes they had talked about "after the war." Yulek's father had said that they would first go back to Poland to see if anyone had returned, then they would leave for Palestine. Yulek considered this his father's last will and testament. And yet month after month for nearly two years he had put off making the trip. At first he was too deeply involved with the training camp, where his group of young people was being taught to form a kibbutz once in Palestine. Later there had been no money for the trip.

Once, on one of the many dark, hopeless nights before his death, Yulek's father told him about his aunt Malka. It was then that Yulek understood the secret of the letter and of the stamp that he mustn't mention to anyone.

As they lay shivering from cold on their joint cot in an airless bunk, his father laughed, perhaps the only time he did so in the month before he died. He told

Yulek how Aunt Malka had studied in Warsaw and gone to London, where she met a young Englishman who wanted to marry her. It took repeated inquiries from the family to find out that he was a Christian. Pleading letters were sent, to no avail, and Malka's father decided to travel to London and retrieve his renegade daughter. Before he could set out, however, a letter arrived with news of her marriage. Yulek's grandfather swore never to think of Malka again and forbade all mention of her name. But Yulek's parents felt too close to Malka to cut all ties with her. It was the one time in his life that Yulek's father lied to Grandfather. Once a year Yulek's mother sent Malka a long letter telling her about the family, and once a year Malka wrote back about herself. Yulek's father never wrote or even read these letters, but he was kept informed of them and sent messages to Malka through his wife. Malka's letters were not delivered to the house. The postman would inform them with a wink that registered mail had arrived, and Yulek's mother would pick it up at the post office.

Yulek's father could not remember Malka's address. He only knew her husband's name and that she lived in London. Perhaps he had had a premonition that no one from their large family would survive the war, and wanted Yulek to know that he still had one living relative. He may even have known that he was dying and been frightened by the thought of leaving Yulek alone. Yet talking with his father about Aunt Malka that night had not made her any more tangible to Yulek. The whole civilized world was so unreal that Yulek did not take the story seriously and forgot the Englishman's name. All his efforts to remember it after the war were in vain.

From his native town Yulek traveled to Lódz, where he checked the lists of the Jewish community for anyone from his family. There was no one. With some of the money given to him for the house he bought a watch, a coat, and a pair of good shoes. Then he contacted the Zionist underground and was assigned to a group leaving Poland via a train for Zabrze. Before setting out, a member of the group changed what remained of Yulek's money for dollars, and Yulek sewed them into his new coat. After a day of getting organized in Zabrze, the group traveled to a Czech border town called Nahod. Yulek was surprised to see that the police on both sides of the border knew the group's leaders, who must have paid them off in advance. They did not bother to check documents or ask questions, although they did search baggage thoroughly. Soon afterward the group set out for Bratislava, where it stayed for a few days in some wooden shacks.

Yulek's group was composed of young Polish Jews on their way to Italy. It reminded him of the group he had joined after the war. It even had its own "Yulek," who took charge of everything, and its own "Robert," the young man who changed everyone's Polish money and handled shady transactions. The girls too fit the mold — a nice girl, a selfish girl, a stupid girl, and a girl who did her best to keep up everybody's spirits. Yet Yulek did not share in the camaraderie and optimism. His trip to Poland had left him feeling depressed.

In Vienna they were housed in a palatial building whose odor and interior indicated that it had served as a war hospital. Yulek and his new friends went to spend a day on the town, and since they had no money, he treated them. Everyone assumed that he was rich, and he told no one where his dollars had come from.

A few days later they arrived in a transit camp in Austria, and from there they crossed the Alps at night, taking the Brenner Pass into Italy. Yulek was still not his old self. He went through the motions — he stood, he walked, he talked — but it was all without really being there. It was as if he were someone else watching himself and giving or withholding permission for what he did. He knew what was expected of him and carried it out without feeling. And yet he remembered how excited he had been a year and a half ago, the first time he had made this journey with Robert and the others.

The group was not alone. There were some older DPs — displaced persons — with bundles and packages, and some families with children. Yulek helped them to carry their things and lent a hand in difficult spots. He even carried an eight-year-old girl on his back for several hours. It took a whole night to cross the pass. At sunrise they arrived in a small village, where Jewish Brigade trucks disguised as American army vehicles were waiting for them. Yulek had met members of the brigade before, but for the others it was a dream come true, a first, worshipful encounter with soldiers from

Palestine. Real Jewish soldiers, not the kind you heard about in jokes!

Yulek handed the girl to her parents, who couldn't stop thanking him. Her mother said, "Young man, I'll never forget you until my dying day."

They said goodbye and boarded one of the trucks while Yulek watched from afar. The child was lifted up first, and her mother clambered after her and was handed the family's bundles by her husband.

Suddenly Yulek knew what the matter was. For the first time, he was mourning. Until now, throughout the years of being separated with his father from the rest of his family, he had been busy just staying alive. He had wanted to survive at all cost, even if no one else did, because someone had to live to tell the story. To bear witness. Now, it was as though a chapter in his life had finally closed and he could grieve at last for his childhood and for all the people he had loved and had been close to.

The trucks had canvas tops. When all were aboard the soldiers fastened them and warned the passengers not to make noise. They set out. Yulek did not stay with them for long. After traveling half a day he got off at a town and took a train "home."

2.
Robert

That evening Yulek arrived in the villa from which he had set out for Poland. Warmly he hugged his friends — one of them, Rivka, had tears in her eyes. She was an energetic type who had a crush on Yulek and paid him back for ignoring her advances by constantly teasing him with a mixture of humor and anger.

"She thought you weren't coming back," said Robert with a wink. Without a word Rivka tried pouring a glass of water over him. But Robert was on guard and kept from getting wet.

Yulek was brought up-to-date. Quarrels had broken out in his absence which no one was able to patch up. A new group of youngsters had arrived and the villa was overflowing, but they had been promised that some of them would be shipped out within a month to a new camp on the sea, and from there to Palestine. Robert, Yulek, Rivka, and Rivka's friends, the two sisters Bella and Frieda, were all on the list to depart.

"Will you come?" asked Yulek.

Robert shrugged. "I'll see."

"What's the problem? You don't think you can cut deals in Palestine too?"

"Of course I can. But it's a poor country, and the opportunities are limited."

"That's true," said Yulek. "But on the other hand,

you'll be getting in on the ground floor. You'll be part of something new, one of the first."

"Maybe" was all Robert said.

One of the girls came running up to them. "Hey, there's a journalist here!" She pulled them after her out of the dining room.

The journalist had been sent by the Jewish Agency in Palestine and was still huffing and puffing after climbing on foot from the village below. He wanted to photograph a group of young Jewish DPs who dreamed of the Land of Israel. He planned to publish the picture in newspapers all over the world to show how wrong the British were in keeping the survivors of the Holocaust out of Palestine.

Although Yulek was tired and wanted to sleep, Rivka took him by the arm and pulled him along. As always, her warm touch felt both good and guilt-provoking. It was nice to know that someone, especially a girl his age, cared about him and wanted so much to be good to him that she would have liked nothing better than to prove her devotion by nursing him through a fever. He couldn't say that he didn't enjoy her attentions: always seeing to it that his shirts and pants were freshly pressed, and touching or putting an arm around him whenever she could. It was human warmth, and he liked her even if she was sometimes bossy. And yet knowing that he could never love her made him feel so uncomfortable that he sometimes drove her away or began to argue with her over trifles, leaving her hurt and close to tears. Often, however, he responded to her overtures and simply tried not to think of the fact that he was promising her more than he could offer.

Now, returning dejectedly from his hard, disappointing journey, Yulek wondered whether it wasn't merely stubbornness that made him keep Rivka at arm's length. A bit of love and tenderness was just what he needed. Yielding, he went with her to join the group of youngsters striking theatrical poses for the photographer.

Afterward they returned to the dining room, where the tables were already neatly set. Yulek, Robert, Rivka, and the two sisters sat together. Yulek opened his coat lining and proudly returned the money he had borrowed from Robert. He even restrained himself and said nothing when Robert smirked at hearing what he had gotten for the house. Robert hadn't meant to wound him; it was Yulek's naiveté that he loved best of all. And besides, after listening to Yulek's story he agreed that his friend had been lucky to get anything at all. The whole episode could just as easily have ended with a bullet in the brain.

Yulek liked Robert too, even though they were very different. Sometimes he teased Robert by saying that he should stay in Italy and become a Mafia boss. Yulek had met Robert in the concentration camp while his father was still alive, yet he had kept his distance because of his father's warnings that Robert was in thick with the kapo, the Ukrainian section head who did the Nazis' dirty work. But if this was so, Robert eventually fell out of favor. One day he was whipped and deprived of his daily bread ration for not tipping his hat when the kapo passed. Although Robert lay groaning in his bunk, Yulek's father was quickly fading that day, and Yulek had no thought for anyone else. When his father died, Yulek shut the dead man's eyes and suddenly noticed Robert's stare. He saw the object of it too, and in an act of rare generosity he unwrapped his father's bread ration from its rag, took one big bite out of it, and handed the rest to Robert. It didn't occur to him at the time that he had saved Robert's life.

As the British army approached, the Germans emptied the camp and marched the prisoners away. Most of them died en route of hunger, cold, exhaustion, or a bullet, but Robert had gotten wind of the evacuation from another kapo he had befriended. The man hid Robert and Yulek in the basement of the camp office until the British arrived. Despite their friendship, Yulek never asked Robert about his relations with either of the kapos, both thoroughly nasty men.

After the liberation, Robert had many opportunities to demonstrate his talents. Appointed by the occupation authorities to confiscate food from the German villagers for the camp survivors and the British army, he grew rich by taking bribes from farmers to expropriate their neighbors' animals and harvests instead of their own.

Yulek, however, hurried to establish contacts with emissaries from Palestine and got together a group of youngsters who wished to settle there. A soldier from the Jewish Brigade put him in touch with an organization in charge of smuggling immigrants into the country. The group needed money. Robert said that this was no problem. To Yulek's amazement, he raised his prices, and the bribes now sufficed for the whole group.

Soon after that their ways parted. Yulek and his group set out for Brussels, while Robert stayed behind to make more money from black market transactions between the Russian and Anglo-American zones of occupation. It was only in a large United Nations refugee camp in Rome, which was the youth group's next stop, that they met again. There Yulek found Robert under arrest for forging German concentration camp numbers on the wrists of DPs to enable them to get special benefits. He and two friends managed to extract Robert from the custody of the Italian police and bring him to the safe house of their villa. Robert couldn't thank him enough. It was thus that their friendship was renewed in spite of the fact that they thought so differently about nearly everything.

Money was all Robert cared about. The dream of building a Jewish state seemed laughably naive to him, and he thought it ridiculous of Yulek's group to work for next to nothing for local Italian farmers in preparation for life on a kibbutz. Yulek, who believed unquestioningly in his duty to take part in the rebirth of the Jewish people in its land, overlooked Robert's faults and hoped that once in Palestine he would be infected with the general spirit of idealism. Of course, it was not at all certain that Robert intended to go there, for even after being rescued by Yulek and appointed group treasurer, he made it clear that he would put his own interests first. Still, the group was definitely better off with him in it.

The villa was a mansion with three floors and thirty rooms that stood on a hill a few kilometers away from a picturesque Italian town. The Jewish Agency had rented it for groups of young immigrants like Yulek's, and Yulek had stayed behind with Robert to administer it after his initial group had moved on. Robert had quickly turned it into a lucrative enterprise. The basic idea was simple: whenever a group of DPs departed for Palestine, it left its UN ration cards behind, and as Robert acquired more and more food with these, he was able to sell more and more of it to the Italian townspeople at a handsome profit.

The boys from the villa worked for local farmers and craftsmen. They were supposed to be learning a trade, and their earnings went into a common kitty. Most of the girls worked in the villa, cooking and cleaning. Each of them was in charge of several boys, whose rooms they tidied and whose clothes they laundered and pressed. Generally, they were happy to "stay home" and do this, though some preferred working elsewhere and were allowed to do so.

It wasn't just the money he made that kept Robert with them. He liked the group's company, especially that of the girls, who were fond of him too. He was generous with his profits and often treated them all to the movies. Rivka in particular was close to him and tried using him to make Yulek jealous. It didn't work, but after Robert told Yulek how miserable he was making her, Yulek decided to have a talk with her. He told Rivka that he liked her and valued her friendship, but that this wasn't enough to make him fall in love with her. Looking back, he wasn't sure if the talk had made things better or worse. He couldn't tell if he had caused her to give up or, on the contrary, to be more in love with him than ever.

"You're afraid of women, that's your problem," said Robert, laughing. "Why don't you come to town with me one night. There's this place there . . ."

Yulek wanted no part of it.

The groups kept coming and going while the five of them remained. Yulek was the manager, Robert the treasurer, Rivka the housemother, and the two sisters, Bella and Frieda, her assistants. They became a tightly knit family.

For a while, whether out of loneliness or to prove Robert wrong, Yulek began to take up with Bella. But although they went into town a few times for a movie or a walk, not even the beautiful landscape and the approach of a ravishing spring could make Yulek fall in love. He did, however, succeed in reopening Rivka's wounds with a vengeance. She had a huge fight with Bella. Yulek decided to give up women altogether and ended up hurting everyone's feelings. Love, he decided, could not be willed into existence. It had to come by itself. He didn't realize how soon it would.

3.

A Surprising Discovery

Melanie sat pensively by the table. Mary had begun to clear the dishes, and her husband, Lord James Faulkner, had gone down the hall to their home library. *James must have forgotten something there,* Melanie thought — *perhaps the material for tomorrow's trial that he was supposed to prepare last night.* She smiled to herself. He might seem severe and punctual, but often his true character, which was not a little lax and mischievous, showed through.

It had been a mild winter, and London bustled with postwar reconstruction. Although the fighting had ended two years before, the hectic rebuilding still went on. And yet soon after Germany's surrender, James had said to her a bit sadly with his usual political foresight, "We've won the war, but I'm afraid we're about to lose the empire."

Indeed, Prime Minister Attlee had already announced the granting of independence to India. Would Palestine be next? Melanie and her husband often talked about it. She could not imagine a handful of Jewish pioneers turning back the assaults of the country's Arabs, who were supported by Arab states and their rulers, such as King Farouk of Egypt and Emir Abdullah of Transjordan. This had worried her even more since finding out that a good friend of hers from Warsaw University, with whom she was now in touch again, had survived the war and was living on a kibbutz. Melanie's husband, though, thought that the Jews would hold their own.

"I had several occasions to observe them when I was in Palestine during the war, Melanie, and I daresay they'll yet surprise us all."

Although she wanted to believe him, Melanie was pessimistic. After all that had happened to the Jews in Europe . . .

She drank her coffee and smoked while watching Mary clean up. Melanie had met James back in the thirties, during her first visit to England. It was all because of Joseph Conrad, the Polish-born author who had left his homeland as a child and spent years in the British merchant marine before becoming a famous English novelist. The first book of his that Melanie came across was *Lord Jim*, followed by *Victory* — both in Polish translation, of course. At first her Orthodox father hadn't allowed her to borrow such "godless books" from the lending library, but once he had agreed to enroll her in the local high school, he had no choice but to put up with it. And while even then he had demanded to see the books she brought home, it had been easy to hide the suspect ones from him. It was Joseph Conrad who had persuaded her to learn English in order to read him in the original.

She finished high school with honors and then, when introduced by her parents to the "good Jewish boy" whom they were determined that she marry, she ran away to Warsaw to study English literature at the university. Much to her surprise, her father soon forgave her and even sent her a monthly allowance. After three years at the university, she decided to fulfill a dream and travel to London. She worked hard for half a year to save enough money for the transportation and a month's stay in the British capital. During her stay she met James.

It happened by sheer accident. How else could a poor Jewish student from Poland have gotten to know one of the most brilliant barristers in the British judicial system? Thinking back on that meeting still made her get up and look at herself in the mirror. Certainly, the face she saw there helped explain it. Whenever she asked him what had made him marry her, he always answered that she had simply bowled him over with her beauty.

Yet although he insisted that she was as beautiful as ever, the first wrinkles were beginning to appear in her skin, and there were gray hairs among the blond ones. Now Melanie turned her back to the mirror and returned to the table, just in time to rescue the ashtray and what was left of her coffee from Mary's quick hands.

"Can I bring you some more coffee, Lady Faulkner?"

"No, thank you, Mary. You can clear the rest of the table. And see if the newspapers have arrived."

Melanie heard Mary's steps descending the stairs. Something fell in the library, and James swore at it. She smiled. Perhaps at his club, men said such things all the time. But his club was out of bounds for her.

Sometimes she believed in fate. It was as if everything were already written somewhere and had to happen the way it did, including her meeting James. He laughed at what he called her superstitions. At most he was ready to acknowledge that there was no such thing as perfect freedom of the will. You could call it fate or blind chance. Either way, you couldn't test it in a laboratory.

They had met in the street as she was coming out of a bookstore that he was entering. He must have been in high spirits, because he was whistling to himself and brandishing his walking stick that now hung on their bedroom wall. Sometimes he would still ask her: "Did it really hurt you that much, or were you just pretending?"

"Why should I have pretended, James?"

"That's the woman's role, to be the victim, isn't it?"

"James, I am a liberated woman," Melanie had to remind him each time.

The walking stick had struck her in the leg. It was metal-tipped, and even he had to admit that being poked in the bone with it couldn't be much fun. Perhaps he kept asking her about it only because he liked to remember that day.

He gave her his arm, led her back into the store, and helped her sit down. Then he sat beside her and apologized. He offered to make her a compress with his handkerchief. A warm rush passed over her when their eyes met.

That was how it had begun.

James Faulkner stuck to his guns despite fierce opposition from Melanie's family and the teasing of his fellow jurists who had never seen her. And she stuck to hers. Her parents renounced her and even sat in mourning, as Orthodox Jews do for family that marries out of the faith, even though she had not converted. Only her brother and sister-in-law kept in touch with her, and that clandestinely.

After the war Melanie was a persistent visitor to the London office of the Jewish Agency, which kept updated lists of the Jewish survivors of the Holocaust. James called it making the Jewish rounds. Now and then he would inquire: "Melanie, have you made your Jewish rounds recently?"

Undeterred, she went back and forth between this office and that of the London Jewish community, reading the names on the bulletin boards that hung in the long corridors. Not all of the lists were alphabetical, and even those that were she read line by line — just to make sure. Sometimes she did find a name under the wrong letter. It was in this fashion that she came across the name of her old friend Henya Meinmer, thus arousing new hopes. Surely this was a sign to go on looking for more and even closer survivors! At first she dropped by the offices every day. Then once a week. Eventually she took to telephoning first and visiting only when told that new lists had arrived.

In the meantime she wrote Henya a letter and received a long answer bringing her up-to-date on her old friend's life. Henya had lost her husband and two children in the Holocaust and now lived on a kibbutz in Israel, where Melanie was invited to visit. Melanie had actually been interested in kibbutzim ever since she read an article about them in a weekly newsmagazine, and James had promised her that one day they would take a trip to Palestine. He was keen on meeting old army mates he had served with in the Middle East, but tensions there were running so high that he preferred to postpone the trip.

Melanie wrote her old friend about her life in London, about James, and about her unsuccessful search for members of her family. Henya too, though she had returned to Poland at the end of the war and spared no pains looking, had failed to find a single living relative.

Melanie thought of her own visit to the town where she had been born. She was thankful that she had not gone by herself but had been escorted by an official representative of the British ambassador. The looks cast her way were the same as those she remembered from before the war, which had put an end to Poland's Jews but not to the Poles' hatred of them. She knew the local residents were lying when they showed her a burned house and told her that her family had moved into it before being herded off to the ghetto. The former forester, now the local Communist party chairman, swore he had seen her family killed and had even taken her to where they were supposedly buried. But though she had given him some money for a tombstone, she had not believed a word of his story.

In her most recent letter, Henya had written that she had married a kibbutz member and was pregnant. In reply Melanie sent her all her best wishes. She and Henya were the same age, thirty-seven. She told James about it and got no reaction.

Melanie was jealous of Henya. When the war broke out, they had both been young and full of plans that they had been forced to postpone. And who could have imagined that the war would go on for so long? James served for three years with the British army in Egypt, and Melanie worked as a volunteer in a London hospital. Every month or two James flew to London on some mission. Naturally, they put off having a baby until after the war. But by the time it was over, they decided they were too old to be parents.

Mary came back with the newspapers, and Melanie sighed. Once again she had to shield the ashtray and coffee cup from Mary's grasp. Her eyes fell on a photograph of some youngsters on the front page of the *Jewish Chronicle*. The headline read: "Youths Saved from Camps Wait in Italy."

Melanie read on. "The British and world Jewish communities are up in arms over His Majesty's government's barring of Palestine to Jewish immigrants. How much longer will our people's saving remnant be denied admission to its promised land?"

She could hear Attlee, the prime minister, laugh as he spoke to her with a wink at one of his many cocktail parties. "Promised, eh? Not by us, Lady Faulkner."

Melanie squinted at the photo. Suddenly she jumped to her feet, then sat down again. "It can't be!" she told herself out loud in an excited voice. "It can't be . . ."

She rose again and went hurriedly to the drawer in which James kept his stamp collection. Rummaging frantically through it, she found a magnifying glass and raced back to the table.

"Is something the matter, ma'am?" Mary asked worriedly from the doorway.

"No, Mary, nothing. You may go now."

Melanie feverishly spread the paper on the table and leaned over it with the magnifying glass. Then she removed her reading glasses and looked again. But the magnifying glass made everything too big and blurry; it was better with her reading glasses alone. A minute later she hurried to her bedroom, where she kept an album of family pictures in her night table. It had snapshots of her parents, her two sisters, and her older brother, Artur. There were also pictures of herself as a two-year-old and others of her with her parents when she was five or six. She remembered their visit to Pan Kirszenbojm the photographer, who made them stand for a very long time in front of his strange machine while moving their heads this way and that, until he finally disappeared underneath a black cloth and her torments were over. There was also a high school graduation picture of thirty Jewish boys and two Jewish girls, of whom she was one.

Melanie snatched the album and returned to the dining room. The newspaper and magnifying glass were gone.

"Mary!"

Mary came running down the stairs from an upstairs room.

"Yes, ma'am?"

"Where are the newspapers?"

"I thought . . ." Mary's voice trailed off. "I simply put it all away, ma'am. I'm so sorry . . ."

Melanie put down the album and retrieved the paper and magnifying glass. "Just a minute," she called to Mary, who was heading back up the stairs. She opened the album and stared hard at a photograph of her brother. This time the magnifying glass definitely helped. The photograph had been taken when he was about sixteen, and Melanie studied it at length before turning back to the picture in the paper. She repeated this sequence several times. Then she laid the album alongside the newspaper and handed Mary the magnifying glass.

"Mary, what do you see?"

Mary had no idea what was expected of her.

"Look at this boy in the album. That's right. And now take the magnifying glass and look at this boy in the newspaper."

Mary, who had never used a magnifying glass before, kept moving it back and forth with a frown, until Melanie snatched it away and told her to compare the two boys without it.

"But there are so many boys in this one, ma'am. I'm all confused. Which one do you mean?"

"Please fetch me a pencil from my husband's drawer."

Mary brought a pencil, and Melanie circled one of the boys in the newspaper. "What do you say now, Mary?" she asked.

"What would you like me to say, ma'am?"

Melanie tried to hide her impatience. "I want you to tell me if you think these two boys look alike. That's all. Do they or don't they? Take a good look and don't rush. I want to know what you think."

Mary was an excellent housemaid and adept at guessing what her employers wanted to hear, which was what she generally told them. This time, however, she had no idea what that was.

"Well, it's not the same hair . . ." she began.

"Forget about their hair. And their clothes. Just concentrate on their faces. What do you say?"

A long while went by before Mary said a word. Melanie waited as tensely for her answer as for the verdict of a court.

"Yes, ma'am. They're quite similar. Is that all right?"

"Yes, Mary, it's all right. But it would also be all right if you said they weren't. What's your opinion?"

Mary studied the two photographs again.

"I still think they're quite similar, ma'am."

Melanie let out a deep breath. "Thank you. You may go now. Has my husband gone out?"

"Lord Faulkner is just putting on his coat."

Melanie ran to the front door and called, "James! James! One minute!"

He stepped back into the hallway. "Yes, dearest. Is anything the matter?"

He put his briefcase and hat on the table and went over to her. Melanie tried to control herself. Her husband's critical eye might yet send her hopes crashing.

"There's something I want you to look at. I can't believe it, but . . . here, you tell me."

She handed him the magnifying glass and pointed wordlessly at the two photographs. James glanced at them and then sat down and studied them closely with the same expression of aloof interest that she knew so well from the courts.

"This is a photo of your brother, Albert, isn't it? And this?" He looked at the newspaper. "Was it you who circled this face? What's on your mind?"

"James, it's time you remembered that my brother's name was Artur. And now tell me what you think."

He debated for a moment before saying, "Yes, dearest, there is a definite resemblance. I'm sorry, but I must be off or I'll be late."

He kissed her lightly and went. Melanie remained at the table, lost in thought. Now and then she glanced at the two photographs. After a while she called for Mary and uncharacteristically requested another cup of coffee and an ashtray.

Melanie returned home tired after a day spent running about town. It was afternoon. James wouldn't be home until suppertime. She hadn't the patience to wait, so she tried getting him on the phone. He wasn't in his office. Nor was he in court. She tried his club and was told he hadn't arrived yet. She left him a message, and half an hour later he called back.

"Were you looking for me, dearest?"

Usually she never bothered him during the day. Even urgent matters were put off until evening, which was why he sounded worried now.

"It's about those photographs."

"I'd hate for you to be disappointed. There's un-doubtedly a resemblance. Even a great one. But you do know, my dear Melanie, that we all descend from Adam and Eve."

"Listen, James. Something tells me I'm right. The boy is alive. It's a miracle. I'm sure of it. And to think that at this very moment the royal fleet of your government, Britannia's pride, is keeping him from reaching Palestine . . ."

"Dearest," James said soothingly. She knew she was attacking the wrong man. "You know what I think of Attlee's Middle East policies. I've even told him so in plain English. But he's convinced that I'm prejudiced because of you."

She could hear him smile at the other end of the line.

"They're afraid," James continued, "that if the British government opens the gates of Palestine to the refugees, it will lose its impartial status."

"Impartial, imshmartial," said Melanie.

He laughed. He always laughed at the Yiddish that she sometimes injected into their conversations.

"It's just possible that we'll soon be out of this mess. You know that I complimented the foreign minister for his decision to refer the Palestine question to the United Nations. That was less than two weeks ago. Let's wait and see what happens."

"Do you really believe in the United Nations, James?"

"It's the best chance there is. Anyhow, I wouldn't rely on a photograph printed in a newspaper. Perhaps you could get hold of the original."

"I did. I was at the paper. The resemblance is even more astonishing. I asked where in Italy the photograph was taken and was referred to the Jewish Agency. I went there too."

"I see you've had a busy day."

She went on telling her story while he listened patiently. In the end he asked, "If the boy is alive, do you think he knows that *you* are?"

"I'm sure he remembers me. I was his aunt Malka, who went abroad and died there. That's what he was told when he was little. He was just a baby when I left for the university, but I saw him after that too, when I came home to visit. He must have been about eight when I saw him last. It's hard to say whether they would have told him the truth when he was older. I never asked about that in my letters to his mother. But I'm sure that if he had known my present name or address, he would have written long ago."

"You must know his name."

"He was called Yulek. That's a nickname for Julian. Why?"

"It's not very Jewish-sounding."

"Artur was a modern man, James. You might say that he was rather assimilated. And he was very fond of the poems of the Polish poet Julian Tuwim. He tried to fit into his Polish surroundings. Not that it helped him. Or any Jew." She sighed. "He broke off ties with me only because of Father. He always did what Father told him to. But even then he kept in touch. Yes, Julian Goldenberg. If only they'd told me where in Italy the picture was taken. Can you imagine that they refused? I mean, they said they didn't know. I don't believe them, though."

"They refused even though you wore your new hat?" asked her husband over the telephone. She could feel him smile again.

Melanie laughed, her sense of calm restored.

"The people in charge of the illegal Jewish immigration —"

"James, you can't call the return of Jews to their own land illegal."

"I'm sorry, dearest. I was saying that the immigration of Jews to the Holy Land is a highly secret matter. And you're on the wrong side of the fence now, you know. They don't want the locations of their camps made known. The Jewish Agency knows that you're the wife of Lord Faulkner."

She could tell that he was still waiting to hear why she had called. And so she told him.

"They referred me to the Jewish Agency offices in Jerusalem."

He was still waiting.

"James, there's something I must tell you."

"Yes, my dear."

"I've made up my mind to go there."

"To Jerusalem?"

"Yes, James."

"Isn't that overdoing it, dearest? Although on the other hand . . . well, I do trust your intuitions, as illogical as they may seem. I must warn you, though, that you may be in for a disappointment. If you're not prepared for it, it will break your heart. I . . . I can only wish you good luck and do what I can to facilitate matters. I've a friend in Jerusalem, Major Scott. I even believe he's involved in keeping out the refugees. Of course, he's only carrying out orders. And he'll be delighted to help you when you arrive. I rather think you met him once. And I'll ask my secretary to make all the arrangements —"

She uncharacteristically cut him short. "I've already made them, James. I have the tickets."

"Sometimes you surprise me. I hope I'll still find you home this evening."

She laughed with relief. He hadn't opposed her! Once more he had justified her faith in him. He was always there to support her, even when he had to bear the brunt of it. She loved him terribly. She never for a moment forgot how he had stood by their love against his parents and tyrannical grandfather. Not, she thought, that her own father was any less of a tyrant.

"If you should actually manage to bring him here, I hope it will be possible to civilize him after all he's been through in Europe."

"I reckon he's about seventeen years old, James. I'm not at all sure that he'll agree to be a child whom I can bring home with me. At most I can perhaps be his aunt. But that still makes me the person closest to him in the whole world."

"And me, too," said Lord Faulkner.

"Thank you, James," said Melanie with feeling.

"When is your flight?"

"Tomorrow morning."

"You don't merely surprise me sometimes," James said, laughing. "You totally dumbfound me."

"I sometimes dumbfound myself," Melanie admitted.

"What airline flies to Palestine?"

"Imperial Airways."

"Well, at least they've got good planes. Dakota DC3s, if I'm not mistaken. You'll have a long flight, though."

"I know. They told me that even without the stopovers it's twenty hours."

"Stopovers where?"

"Paris, Rome, Athens, and probably Nicosia. But they're all short."

"Yes, just for refueling and letting passengers on and off. I suppose I had better cable Major Scott urgently."

"I'm not sure he can be of much help, James, considering his position."

"Well, I'll let him know that you're coming anyway. Just so he won't be surprised if you drop in."

"If I have time, I'd like to see my old friend Henya too."

For a moment James had no idea whom she was talking about. Then he remembered. "The one who married and went to a kibbutz? Or was it the other way around?"

"I wonder what she's like now," said Melanie pensively. "We were very good friends as students in Warsaw. She was the only person I corresponded with about the two of us."

"That makes me think more highly of her already," James said. And after a pause, he added, "I'll come home early, Melanie."

They might have no children, Melanie thought warmly, but they certainly did have each other.

4.
Theresa

A small old van groaned up the winding path to the top of the hill and reached the gate of the villa. The driver honked. Yulek stepped into the front yard and yelled, "Motke, open the gate!"

Some people thought that Motke was retarded, but it was Yulek's opinion that he was simply out of tune with his surroundings. Yulek, who was the only one ready to share his quarters with Motke, had persuaded Robert to take him in as a third roommate. He was also the only one who didn't call him Hey-Motke.

Motke opened the two wings of the gate, and the van screeched into the yard. Those of the group posted at the villa that day came lazily down from their rooms, yawning and stretching their limbs.

The Italian driver said hello and joked with them. He had learned a few words of Polish, Rumanian, and even Yiddish, and by now the villa occupants could speak a broken Italian. Yulek helped the group unload crates of vegetables from the van.

When they were done, a girl he hadn't seen before, no doubt one of the newcomers, approached the driver and gestured that she'd like a ride into town. As Yulek moved closer, she turned around. His heart skipped a beat. Even when she turned back to the driver he could not take his eyes off her. He had already heard from

Robert that there was a stunning girl in the new group, but since Robert said that about nearly everyone, he hadn't paid any attention.

A window on the second floor opened. Bella and Frieda were standing next to Rivka, who shouted something while pointing at the new girl.

"What's the matter?" asked Yulek. "Is she on duty today?"

Instead of answering, the three girls left the window and soon appeared downstairs. "When we all go to town together at night to see a movie or have a good time, she never wants to come," said Rivka about Theresa, which was the new girl's name. "But whenever she can, she goes there by herself."

Theresa looked about sixteen. She glanced without a word at Yulek and then at the three girls, who were standing there threateningly.

Yulek failed to see what Rivka was so annoyed about. "What's it to you?" he asked.

"Yesterday we discovered what she does there," said Frieda. Bella nodded in confirmation.

"What is it?" asked Yulek, amused.

"You think it's funny?" Rivka answered contentiously. "Here, have a look."

She went over to the unsuspecting Theresa and yanked at the chain around her neck. Theresa defended it. They struggled for a minute until Rivka tugged the chain loose from Theresa's blouse and held it up triumphantly. Swinging from the bottom was a small golden cross. "She goes to church, that's what she does!" Rivka announced.

Theresa snatched the chain back with tears in her eyes. Yulek intervened. "Leave her alone," he said. "She can go to town when she wants and do what she pleases there." He went over to Theresa. "Let me see the chain. Maybe I can fix it for you."

Her bright green eyes had a slight upward slant, giving her an exotic beauty. It was no wonder, thought Yulek, that Rivka had it in for her. Not that the other girls seemed to like her any better.

Yulek could easily imagine where the cross had come from. She wasn't the first youngster he had encountered who had been hidden from the Nazis by a Christian family, or else in a convent or monastery. The younger ones had never even known they were Jewish until the war was over and their relatives or Jewish officials came to retrieve them. This wasn't always simple, as the Christian families often resisted giving up a child they had come to consider their own, and there were wrenching scenes of parting. Though the war had ended, the war's problems had not. Yulek stared at Theresa, trying to guess what her story had been. She stole a quick glance at him, and he felt himself blush. Her cheeks were flushed too.

She took the torn chain back from him and climbed into the seat by the driver.

"She can go where she wants," repeated Yulek. "We'll take it up at the next group discussion."

Hey-Motke opened the gate, and with a roar and a screech the van set off back to town.

"You don't get it," said Rivka. "She doesn't even want to be Jewish. What is she doing here? Why should she come with us to Palestine? Let her go back to Poland! Didn't we suffer from the Catholics enough without having to watch her cross herself all day?"

"You're exaggerating, Rivka," said another girl. "She's someone to feel sorry for. I saw other kids like her in Poland. They get over it. She *is* Jewish, after all. She wouldn't be here if she weren't."

Yulek went off to inspect the kitchen.

"Will you come to a movie with us in town tonight?" Bella called after him.

"Sure," he answered gladly.

The two sisters were nice but not especially pretty. Both were committed Zionists. They thought alike, acted alike, and even looked alike, resembling the women pioneers who had helped found the first Jewish farming villages in Palestine at the end of the last century.

Although Yulek looked for Theresa in the dining room that day, he saw her only the next morning. After a moment of awkward agitation that was new to him, he went and sat down beside her. They exchanged a few polite words. The chain was still around her neck, but there was no telling if the cross was beneath her blouse. He started to ask if she had had it fixed, then thought better of it.

Sitting beside Theresa once might have been considered a coincidence, but Yulek kept it up for several days. One morning Robert joined them. He started a conversation with her, talked and joked with his usual charm, and didn't let Yulek get a word in.

That evening there was a get-together in the dining

room in honor of a new mandolin that Robert had bought the day before. They sang songs in Yiddish, Polish, Russian, and Hebrew, and Robert displayed one more of his many talents by accompanying them on the instrument. He had a fine voice, for which he was forgiven all sorts of shenanigans. It was hard to dislike him for long.

But the next morning Robert beat Yulek to it and sat beside Theresa before him. At first Yulek tried to tell himself that it was nothing; within a day or two, though, he was forced to admit that he had a rival. And if Robert was seriously vying for Theresa, Yulek would be hard-pressed to compete with him. Still, he thought, he would not give up without a fight.

Yulek didn't know what to do. Once upon a time such things were settled by fighting a duel, but nowadays it wasn't so simple. He began to get touchy about what Robert said and stopped deferring to him in all kinds of little things, in the office and in the room that they shared.

The first thing that they quarreled over was Robert's bed, which was often a mess for days on end unless Rivka came to make it — something that hadn't bothered Yulek before but now struck him as unbearable. Next they fought over the light. Robert liked to stay awake at night reading cheap English thrillers, and suddenly the light kept Yulek awake.

"Don't bother me," Robert said. "I'm trying to learn English." He was not yet aware of their changed relationship — or was pretending not to be.

"I wouldn't mind so much if it were Hebrew," snapped Yulek. "I want to sleep. Turn out the light."

"I will not. This isn't your private room."

Yulek rose and turned off the light. Robert rose, turned it back on, and remained standing by the light switch until Yulek pushed him away from it. All at once Yulek realized that he was the stronger of the two. Only the frightened face of Hey-Motke made him stop spoiling for a fight. Hey-Motke was very attached to them both. All his life he had been jeered at and made fun of, and just when he finally had two powerful brothers, they were at each other's throats. Yulek yielded and went back to bed.

Robert turned out the light. Then he asked, "What's up, Yulek? What have I done to you?"

"Nothing," Yulek said. "You just get on my nerves."

Yulek wasn't aware that his anger had to do with Theresa. Duels were a thing of the past, but though not seen the same way, fistfights over a pretty girl were still common.

That week he had to travel with Robert to UN headquarters in Rome. As usual, Robert tried to ride the train without a ticket. This time, though, Yulek had had enough.

"I'm tired of your swindles," he said.

"You didn't mind borrowing the money I made from them when you went to Poland," Robert shot back.

He disappeared, and they did not meet again until the station in Rome.

As they were leaving, a gust of wind blew Robert's

new Italian hat off his head. It fell at Yulek's feet, and Yulek stepped on it. In retrospect it occurred to him that he might have sidestepped the hat, but crushing it made him feel so good that he grinned as he ground his foot into it. A second later the grin turned to a wince as Robert's fist landed in his ribs. Instinctively he struck back with a blow to Robert's face. While curious onlookers began to gather and to egg them on in Italian, Robert clutched his nose with both hands, then stared at the blood on them. The sight of blood quickly calmed down the two boys. Yulek picked up the hat, smoothed it out, and put it back on the head of his friend, who reached for a handkerchief to stanch the bleeding.

They moved away from the disappointed crowd, and Yulek apologized. "I didn't mean it," he said.

"Mean what?" asked Robert, sounding like he had a bad cold.

"To step on your Borselino." There was a trace of mockery in Yulek's voice. "But it was you who threw the first punch."

They entered a café, and Yulek ordered two cappuccinos and some cake.

"This time it's on me," he said when Robert returned from cleaning his face in the washroom.

"You mean it's on the villa."

"Are you starting up again?"

"I'm not starting anything. You only have to think to realize that it's you who keeps trying to pick a fight. You began yesterday with the light. Actually, you began the day before yesterday with the bed. Maybe you'd like to tell me why."

"As a matter of fact, I would. I've really had it with you."

"Why? What have I done?" asked Robert, feigning innocence.

This just made Yulek madder. "Cut the crap! You wanted to have a serious conversation — now be serious."

"All right," said Robert, taking a sip of coffee. He put the cup down and said, "I know. It's because of Theresa."

"That's right," Yulek said.

"I can see you're in love."

"You'd better not ever say that again! Not to me and not to anyone!"

"That just proves how right I am."

"And wipe that grin off your face," Yulek added sternly.

Robert burst out laughing. Suddenly Yulek realized how ridiculous he was and grinned too.

"Robert," he said, "I really am serious. And there's something I want to ask of you. You yourself don't give a damn. For you one girl is as good as another — I've heard you say it yourself. But I'm not that way. And you know this is the first time I've ever felt like this. So keep away from her."

"All right," Robert said. "You're not telling me anything I didn't know. Maybe I started to flirt with her because I was jealous. I didn't want to lose you to her, so I kept trying to come between you. Does that make sense?"

Yulek understood. Robert's frankness came as a surprise, though. He had always felt that there was more to Robert than met the eye — which might have been what made him take to Robert in the first place — but he had never realized how wise his friend was. He would have liked to give him a hug. Instead he held out his hand and they shook, embarrassed by the drama of the gesture.

When they returned to the villa that evening, Theresa wasn't there. They were told that she had decided to leave because the other girls wouldn't stop attacking her.

"How could you let her go off?" exclaimed Yulek.

"How could we have forced her to stay?" Rivka asked.

It was a good question.

"Where did she say she was going?"

"To Rome," said Hey-Motke.

"Did she say she was coming back?"

"No," answered Theresa's roommate. "But she left most of her things here."

"Then it's all right," said Yulek with a sigh of relief.

"She did take her DP card, though," Rivka pointed out.

A day went by, and then another, and Theresa did not return. Yulek went about his business as usual, but his attention was fixed on the front gate. He felt consumed by worry and a dull ache, and he had nightmares from which he awoke to lie in bed listening for Theresa. Once he even went to her room in the middle of the night and quietly opened the door. Her bed was empty.

After seven days there was still no sign of her. Her disappearance was the subject of that week's discussion. Her fellow group members told Yulek that she had run away from another group before, perhaps for the same reasons. Yulek tried to persuade them to be more patient with her when she returned. Time, he said, would solve all problems. Not everyone agreed. Some said that Theresa was simply too much to bear. Robert said nothing.

When the question was put to a vote, Yulek's position won out over a noisy minority's. Since he had to go to Rome on Jewish Agency business anyway, he asked for and was given authority to set out the next day and to try to find Theresa and bring her back.

He and Robert stayed up late that night. After returning on foot from an evening spent in town, they found Hey-Motke fast asleep and snoring loudly. They rolled him over on his side and the snoring stopped, but Yulek couldn't fall asleep. He was thinking of Theresa and of the next day.

"Where will you look for her?" Robert's voice emerged from the dark as though from his own thoughts. "She could have joined up with another youth group by now. Or decided to try to get to America."

"Maybe she just needed to be by herself for a while," Yulek said. "The girls made her pretty miserable."

He lay there thinking about her.

"Sometimes," Robert said, "I tell myself that after I've made enough money, I'll head there myself."

"Where?"

"America."

"So that you can be a Jew in someone else's country again?"

"All of your speeches just make me want more than ever to go where I can live my own life. Who says that we Jews need a country of our own? The Jews in America live well, believe me."

"Yes, but you could have made up your mind to go there a year ago, when we got to our first camp in Padua."

"You know how it is," Robert said. "You get carried along by the current. And I had my little business deals with those American GIs then. That's what paid for your trip to Poland. Where did you think my loan came from?"

"I thought it was from your profits from the villa," Yulek said.

"That was small change," said Robert. "Anyway, while you were gone I was ganged up on and made to promise that I would donate it to the group."

Yulek laughed in the dark. "How come you stayed on?"

"For lack of anything better to do. But sometimes I feel like clearing out and taking off for Rome myself."

"All I have to do to stay focused on the idea of a Jewish state," Yulek said, "is to think of how helpless we were in the ghetto — of my father, who couldn't save his own wife and children."

"You're a true Zionist," Robert told him. "But I promise you that such things could never have happened in America."

"And in Germany they could have?"

"Yes. The Germans are a people of robots. I don't have to tell you that."

Early the next morning Yulek walked into town and took the first train to Rome. When he was through with his business, he began the search for Theresa. He made the rounds of all the Jewish organizations, although there was little chance of finding her there, since it was more likely that she had sought the aid of a Catholic charity. Later he tried the Polish embassy, but its officials were unhelpful and regarded him with suspicion. He had a bite to eat in a trattoria and took the evening train back.

A storm broke as the train approached his stop, and he got off resigned to a soaking. He hadn't walked very far up the road toward the villa when headlights gleamed behind him. Who could it be at such an hour? He frantically flagged down the vehicle, which was an army truck with a soldier and two girls in the cabin. All three had the look of having come from an exceptionally lively party. Yulek clambered into the open back and almost fell when the truck lurched forward as he swung a leg over the tailgate.

There was a bulge in the back of the cabin. When he looked closely he saw that it was the rolled and tied canvas top, stiff and wet from the rain. Without thinking he lifted its flaps and squeezed under, worming his way to a spot where the floor wasn't so wet. Suddenly his hand touched something soft and warm, and there was a frightened shriek.

"*Scusa*," said Yulek in Italian.

The hoarse shriek, most probably a girl's or young woman's, had sounded like the word for Jesus in Polish. And so, this time in Polish, he said again, "Excuse me."

The answer came in Polish too. "I must have fallen asleep," said the voice.

The truck bounced suddenly, throwing both of them so hard against the tarpaulin that they barely managed to regain their balance. As Yulek helped the girl up, he noticed that she was wearing soft woolen gloves.

"How do you keep from falling?" he asked.

"There's a hole in the canvas," she said. "You can stick your hand through it and grab onto the cabin. I must have let go when I fell asleep."

"Excuse me," Yulek said again, in Polish.

He groped in the dark for the hole, stuck his hand through it, and pulled it right back. "It's freezing," he said. "I'd rather lose my balance."

The girl laughed. "That's what I thought at first too."

It didn't take long for Yulek to see what she meant. The truck took a sharp curve, sending him sprawling against the tarpaulin and then back the other way. Now it was she who had to help *him* up. The two of them burst out laughing.

"All right," Yulek said. "I'll hold on."

It was only then that the girl asked, "Is that you, Yulek?"

"Yes, it's me. Theresa?"

It turned out that she had meant to leave the villa for only a day. She had gone to Rome to get away and to visit the Vatican Museum, and she had regretted leaving almost at once but had been too angry at the other girls to turn back. In the museum she felt she was running a fever, sat down to rest in a corner, and passed out. She came to in a Carmelite hospital. Within a few days she recovered, thanked the mother superior for the devoted treatment she received, and set out for the villa determined to return to Rome and join the Carmelites as a novice.

She did not tell Yulek this last part. Skipping over it, she related that, being afraid to walk to the villa in the rain after having been sick, she had stepped into a little restaurant and met two Italian girls and a drunken soldier who turned out to belong to the Free Polish Forces of General Anders. After a while she persuaded the soldier to drive her to the villa. At first all four of them had tried squeezing into the cabin, but the man couldn't drive that way, and though he tried to get rid of the Italians in favor of Theresa, she refused even though she knew it might cost her the ride. But the soldier took it well and let down the tailgate for her to climb onto the back, where she huddled under the tarpaulin.

"The wine they had me drink must have made me sleepy," Theresa said. "I was scared to death when I felt someone touch me."

"So was I," said Yulek with a laugh. "The last thing I imagined was finding you here after looking for you all day in Rome."

"You were looking for me?"

"We thought you weren't coming back. I went to try to find you."

"But how could you have thought that? You must have known that I left all my things."

"Well, I did have business in Rome anyway. But you came up at our last group discussion, and everyone agreed that I should try to bring you back." After a pause he added, "I don't think you'll have any more trouble with the girls."

He hadn't finished the sentence when a new lurch sent them sprawling. It was hard to talk over the roar of the truck, which was now jouncing up the winding, potholed road. Fighting to stay put, they sat in silence until the truck pulled up at the gate of the villa.

They got out and thanked the Polish soldier. He opened the door of the cabin to say something and would no doubt have tumbled out had the two girls not grabbed him by his uniform and pulled him back in.

"I'll come to see you, gorgeous!" he shouted in Polish over the roar of the engine.

The gate of the villa creaked open, and the drowsy figure of Hey-Motke in pajamas, his coat covering his head like a rain hat, emerged from the dark.

5.
In Jerusalem

It wasn't until the next morning, when Melanie stepped out of the King David Hotel in downtown Jerusalem, that she noticed how much damage had been done to the wing of the hotel by the Jewish underground's bomb the previous summer. More than a hundred Englishmen, she recalled, had been killed. For the Jews of Palestine, Great Britain was now the enemy, even though the two had been allies against Nazi Germany a short while ago.

The hotel was surrounded by soldiers and barbed wire. A bellboy hailed a cab for her. The Arab driver was nonplussed at being asked by an English lady to be taken to the Jewish Agency, but apart from the look on his face he expressed no surprise.

Fences and British-manned roadblocks were visible along the way, but the streets appeared quiet. Soon, though, Melanie realized from the roundabout route they were taking that many of them were simply barred to traffic. She paid the driver and found herself facing a building flanked by more soldiers and barriers.

The structure was a handsome one, built in the shape of a horseshoe around a large courtyard. Melanie asked at the gate for the foreign press liaison and was referred by a guard to an office. Although she spoke only Yiddish to keep from arousing suspicion, the fact of having arrived in a taxi was suspect in itself.

The room she was sent to was large and had three desks. Behind them sat two men and a woman. Melanie approached the woman, but she knew no Yiddish and pointed to one of the men. The latter signaled Melanie to have a seat and went on writing something. After a while he looked up and asked what he could do for her. He spoke Yiddish with a heavy Polish accent, and it was not as easy to communicate as she had thought it would be. Eventually she took the newspaper with the photograph from her bag and spread it out on the table.

"My name is Melanie Goldenberg Faulkner," she began. "By a sheer miracle, after two years of looking for survivors from my family, I opened this paper one day and saw my nephew. Here he is!" She pointed to the photo.

The official glanced at her, looked at the picture, and shrugged. "So," he said, "what is it that you want from me?"

"To tell me where this photograph was taken."

"Ma'am, how should I know?" asked the man. "Moyshe!" he called out. "Come over here!"

The second official rose from his desk, leaned over the newspaper, and studied the picture.

"It's an ordinary wire photo," he said. "There's no way of telling."

Melanie was on the verge of desperation. "But someone must know. You don't understand. My whole family was killed in Poland. I have no one left except for this boy."

"I understand you perfectly, ma'am." The official tried to soothe her. "My family was lost there too. My parents, my brothers and sisters . . . everyone. But how can I know where this photograph was taken? I'm sure you can find out from the newspaper in London. Why don't you write to them?"

"Because I've just come from London. I was told there to turn to you in Jerusalem. I was told that only here —"

"What do you mean, you just came from London?"

"I live there. Didn't anyone ever tell you that Jews live in London?"

"I'm aware of the fact." He gave her a fresh look. "Do you speak Polish too?"

"Of course. I studied at the university in Warsaw."

They exchanged a few polite words in Polish, and the official's confidence was won. The second official stopped working and began to listen too. In the end the first official turned to him and asked, "Moyshe, what do you say?"

"It's all right with me" was the answer.

"We have a photography archive," said the first official. "If your picture is in it, we may be able to help you."

He led her to a room and began to rummage in a metal file cabinet.

"It's a new picture," Melanie said. "It must have been taken recently."

The official took out a large envelope, poured its contents onto an empty desk by the window, and helped Melanie go through them. But although she looked closely at every single photograph, her nephew was not in any of them.

"Don't tell me I came all the way from London for nothing!" she exclaimed.

"Maybe there are more recent photographs that haven't been filed yet," said the official, thinking out loud. "Wait here a minute."

Melanie lit a cigarette and went to stand by the window, midway between hope and despair. She heard footsteps approaching in the corridor and tried to guess what they meant. They were quick, as if the person they belonged to was hurrying with good news. The official entered with another envelope. She put out her cigarette, and they began to look again. One of the photographs caught her attention. It was a large shot of some young men and women sitting around a table in a dining room. She examined their faces one by one and suddenly saw a face like the one she was looking for, though it was hard to tell because it was out of focus. She turned the photograph over and read aloud in Italian from the back of it.

"Now I remember!" said the official excitedly.

He went back to the file cabinet and retrieved a smaller envelope with a place name written on it, from which he took out a batch of photographs that he handed to Melanie. In no time she found the one that had been in the newspaper. "This is it!" she cried. "Where was it taken?"

"Let's go back and ask Moyshe," said the official. "He's sure to know."

And Moyshe did. The place, he explained to Melanie, was a Zionist training camp some eighty kilometers north of Rome, through which many youth groups passed. Each studied Hebrew while there and found work in the area.

"Do you have a list of the names of the young people who are there now?" asked Melanie hopefully.

"No," said Moyshe. "I'm afraid not."

"We're given their names only when they arrive in Palestine," said the first official. "And as you know, ma'am, that's something that your English government is doing its best to prevent."

"Yes, I know," said Melanie. "I'll have to go to Italy. I'd like to thank you very much. I only hope . . . well, that it really is Yulek."

"You sounded so sure that it was," said the official.

"It's not as simple as all that. I left home when he was a small child. I only recognized him in the newspaper because he looks just like my brother. He always did, even as a baby."

She took out a snapshot of her brother. Moyshe looked at it. "Yes," he said. "There's definitely a resemblance."

"And you came all the way here from London on the basis of this?" asked the first official.

"Yes," Melanie answered. "It has to be he. It has to be! May I have the original photograph?"

"I can order a copy for you, but it will take a week or two."

"But I have to take the first flight to Italy!"

"Moyshe, what do you think?"

Moyshe kept silent. The official thought for a moment and said, "All right. I'll give you the photograph and order another one for the archive."

"Is there a charge for it?"

"There's no charge, but donations are always welcome."

Melanie took out a pound note and slipped it into a collection box extended to her. "It has to be Yulek," she whispered to herself.

"You never found his name on any lists of survivors?" asked the official.

"No."

"I hope . . . I'll write you a letter to our people in Italy, just in case. It's not every day that someone comes all the way from England."

The official wrote a few words on a piece of paper, put it in an envelope, and handed this to Melanie.

"I'll never forget how helpful you've been," she said with feeling. "Really, I can't thank you enough."

"Let me know if you find him. My name is Yitzchak Fishler."

"I promise," said Melanie. They shook hands and she left.

6.
The Beginning of the End

There was great excitement in the villa. The long-awaited moment had arrived. On the bulletin board was a list of those chosen to head south on the first leg to Palestine. Each of them was allowed to take twenty kilograms of personal belongings. The departure date was that evening. Yulek unsuccessfully scanned the list for the name of Theresa Ostrowska. That must have been the name given her by her Christian family, he thought. Did she have another, Jewish one? The thought caused him a moment's sadness, because he liked the name Theresa so much. He hurried to the girls' wing and knocked on the door of her room. He had never been in it before, except for the time he had searched for her when she ran away to Rome. The girls were packing amid great disorder.

"Are you all going?" asked Yulek as his glance met Theresa's smile.

"Yes," answered her two roommates.

Just then, from the next room, he heard Rivka call out, "Don't worry! Your Christian is coming along too."

Yulek went to the doorway and said sternly, "You promised me you'd cut that out."

"I'm sorry," Rivka said. "I didn't mean anything bad by it. You can ask her. We're friends now. What about Robert?"

"Robert is on the list also," answered Yulek. It suddenly struck him that Motke wasn't.

The large group set out on foot at twilight. An hour and a half's easy downhill walk brought the excited youngsters to the main road, where they waited for several army trucks with British markings. The soldiers wore British uniforms, although they spoke Hebrew. They handed out K rations and blankets, told everyone to climb aboard, and shut the canvas flaps behind them.

The southward journey in the closed trucks took many

hours. Once or twice they stopped to rest in deserted spots where they would not attract attention. Whenever they did, they went to the "bathroom" by command: "All the girls to the left, all the boys to the right!"

It was dark, and they talked in tense, expectant whispers. Yulek sat next to Theresa. Since they were all packed together, no one could gossip about the two of them sitting so close to each other. And yet, though it seemed the obvious thing to do, he refrained from putting his arm around her for fear of scaring and losing her. Something told him that he had to be extracautious. Although a part of her responded to him with laughter, tender looks, and bodily warmth as long as he did not go too far, there was another, unspoken part that seemed to hold nervously back. Yulek tried to explain it to himself in terms of her convent education.

The news that they were striking camp had come as a surprise, a mere two days after he and Theresa had hitchhiked up the hill in the rain. Except for once in the empty dining room, when they were both on cleanup duty, they hadn't had another chance to talk. He had so much to tell her that it almost annoyed him to have to spend time preparing to leave the villa. It was the first time he had felt like telling anyone about his wartime experiences and about his mother, father, sisters, and childhood in their little Polish village. Still, setting out for Palestine was more important.

In the early morning they reached their first destination. Stiff from the trucks, they were greeted by the salty smell of the sea and marched to a long Quonset hut. Yulek was able to make out the coast a few dozen yards away beyond some trees, as well as another, similar hut and a few light-colored tents. No one was visible besides their guides. They rolled out mattresses on the floor and fell asleep.

When they awoke, they were given hot tea and crackers and told they would have to wait a few days for their ship. There was an old Jeep for supplies and emergencies, and only the driver and his escort were allowed to take it into town. Word had been spread throughout the area, they were informed, that they were a transshipment of mental patients. With a perfectly straight face the man briefing them added that anyone wishing to stroll along the seashore or gather driftwood there for the cooking stoves had better make sure to act oddly and to talk to himself or wave his arms. In the evening, when it grew dark, they would practice boarding the ship.

"Is it here already?" asked someone excitedly.

"No," was the answer. "We have a special mockup of it. You can see it if you go outside. The actual ship will have to anchor offshore. This isn't exactly a well-equipped port."

Most of them were too tired to go outside. Yulek and Theresa were given permission to look for driftwood. It was a lovely day, and the blue sea that stretched all the way to distant Palestine gave them the feeling that their long wanderings were about to come to an end. They approached a strange wooden structure built to resemble the side of a ship and stared at the ladders and ropes hanging down from it.

"Scary, isn't it?" said Theresa.

They set out along the seashore, taking care to wave their arms and jump about insanely, which reduced them to a state of helpless laughter. Theresa wasn't sure if madwomen collected seashells, and Yulek didn't know either, although he couldn't see why not. In the end they found a hidden place among some rocks. At long last they were by themselves.

Yulek lay down in the sand. Theresa sat next to him, playing with some shells she had found and arranging them by color and shape.

"Do you think I could make holes in them and string them?" she asked.

Yulek reached out for a shell and their hands met. The contact was electric. Theresa's cheeks reddened. She pulled back her hand, and the shell fell onto the sand.

Yulek couldn't look at her enough. He felt swept away by her high forehead, her deep green eyes with their hint of a Tartar slant, her finely pointed chin, her delicate yet not overly thin lips that bared perfect teeth when she smiled, lighting up her face like a dawn sky.

"I have to tell you something, Yulek," said Theresa, swallowing hard. "I'm not going to Palestine for the same reasons that you are."

Yulek was startled. "Then why are you going?" he asked.

"I want to be a nun in Jerusalem," Theresa said in a low voice, as if afraid the sea and sky might hear. "I took a vow in the convent."

"What kind of a vow?"

"That if I lived through the war, I'd become a nun."

"In Palestine?"

"No. But that's where my mother superior told me to go."

Yulek's heart was in his throat. *Anything but that,* he thought. He tried picturing her in a long black robe, a white coif on her head like a Polish nun's. She seemed so beautiful even then that he was overwhelmed by sorrow.

She had undone her thick brown braid, which she usually wore wrapped around her head or hanging down her back in the Polish style, and had let her hair blow in the wind. It gave her the look of a wild fairy creature.

He knew why he couldn't let her be a nun. It wasn't to save her for the Jewish people. It was to save her for himself. He looked back at her and said sarcastically, "The Poles would prefer their Jewish nuns to live elsewhere, is that it?"

It struck home. Theresa's chin trembled. Yulek imagined her in her novice's robe, facing the mother superior in a large cold hall, or in some long dim corridor, the same tremor in her chin as the news was broken to her that she would have to leave Poland. He would have given anything, done anything, eaten the very sand he was sitting on, to take back his mockery and restore the calm to her face. But had it never occurred to her that she would one day be told to leave the convent?

Theresa sat thinking. She remembered that day well. She had done her best not to cry. She had had a sense of foreboding even before being summoned to the mother superior, when a little truck had appeared at the convent's gates and strange-looking men with sacks on their backs had climbed down from it. She knew at once that the summons had to do with them and with the war being over.

The mother superior spoke to her about the difficult times the convent was going through. Theresa didn't have to be told. They had gone hungry throughout the war, especially in the last year. The Jews, said the mother superior, knew where their children had been hidden. In fact, the men on the truck had come with a list of the children. That was how Theresa found out that there were three other Jewish girls in the convent, one of them brought there as a baby. She was dumbfounded.

"If I had known this was going to happen," said the mother superior, "I would have smuggled you all out of here. But they were smart. They took me by surprise, and they have guards posted at all the exits."

She told Theresa that the Jews had brought flour and rice in the sacks, as well as money.

"It's too large a sum for us to refuse," she said. "And when you get to the holy city of Jerusalem, Theresa, no one can keep you from becoming a nun there. Please write to me. Perhaps one day you'll be a mother superior like me. Here's a letter of recommendation. I've written it in French. It will open the gates of any convent for you."

"I respected her decision," said Theresa to Yulek after a long silence. "I loved her and understood that she had to do what was best for everyone. The Jews gave the nuns a lot of food and money."

"Yes, they got a good price for you," Yulek felt like

saying, but he didn't want to sadden her even more. He knew that deep down — too deep down to admit it even to herself — Theresa suspected the mother superior of not trusting her, of not believing that she would remain a good Catholic after the war.

All the way to Italy, each time she lay crying silently into her pillow at night, Theresa had reassured herself that she was going to Palestine to be a nun. It was the only way of making that far-off, frightening country seem near and comforting. Whenever she could, she slipped away to a church to pray. In Rome, where she had caught a glimpse of the pope amid a crowd of worshipers, she solemnly renewed her vow. And yet, though she wouldn't have put it this way, she felt the need to do so only because her determination had already been shaken.

"Didn't you realize that some day someone would come to take you from the convent?"

"I didn't think that there were any Jews left. I thought I was the last one."

"Theresa," asked Yulek, desperately trying to get through to her, "don't you ever think of your parents?" The idea of Theresa as a nun alarmed him. He racked his brain for ways to reason with her, as if logic had anything to do with it.

"My parents must have been killed," Theresa said. "Otherwise they would have come for me themselves."

"Suppose they had. What would have happened to your vow then?"

Her chin trembled again, making him want fiercely to protect her. He sat leaning against a rock while she scanned his face as if looking for the answer there.

"You know that your parents put you in the convent only to save your life," he said. "And you know that they meant to come for you when the war was over. Imagine that they could see and hear you now. If they were religious Jews, they might even wish you hadn't lived."

"How could they see me? Don't be childish."

"I thought Catholics believed in Heaven."

"Do you hate Catholics, as Rivka and Robert do?" Theresa asked.

"I can't possibly," said Yulek. "My own aunt married a Christian."

He told Theresa about his aunt Malka, his account based partly on his memories of her and partly on the stories his father told in the concentration camp. She listened closely.

"My grandparents sat in mourning for a week, as if she had died. Afterward we weren't allowed to mention her name. And she wasn't even baptized."

"Then how were they married?"

"I really don't know. Maybe in a civil ceremony. There are countries where you can be married by a justice of the peace. Even if she has become a Christian, I wouldn't stop talking to her because of it, but for you to go now and become one because your parents hid you in a convent — that would be like betraying them."

"Anything else would make me a liar," said Theresa. "Does your aunt have children?"

"She didn't have any before the war."

"How old is she now?"

"Close to forty, I should think."

"Would you like to find her?"

"I'd love to," Yulek said. "Do you know what it's like to know that there is still someone alive who's close to you, who knew your parents, the home you grew up in, you yourself as a child?"

"I know." Theresa sighed. After a while she asked, "Suppose she really did become a Christian. Would that be a reason not to look for her?"

Yulek thought for a minute. "No," he answered.

She said nothing. From afar came the voice of someone from their group who was acting a bit more crazy than was called for. Or perhaps that was precisely what was called for. Then there was silence again, and they heard only the boom of the sea.

"The mother superior was good to me," Theresa said. "I thought my becoming a nun would make her happy. And she did hug and kiss me when I told her I wanted to be one. That was something she hardly ever did. I became a Catholic after everyone from my town was killed. I didn't think it mattered anymore. I never thought I'd meet another Jew again. I thought the only ones alive were girls like me, in the convents."

There was a long silence.

"I want you to promise me one thing," said Yulek at last.

She sat listening.

"Don't tell anyone that you were baptized. No one has to know. All it amounts to is a few words and some water that was sprayed on you. By the time we reach Palestine, you may change your mind."

"I may," whispered Theresa. She picked up the sea-shell she had dropped before.

"When you get there and see how everyone is Jewish," Yulek said enthusiastically, "— the farmers, the bus drivers, everyone — you'll think differently. There's no knowing now what it will be like." He thought for a moment and said, "Have you ever considered why you wear that cross all the time?"

"It's because I believe in Jesus," said Theresa in a small voice.

"It's not only that," said Yulek. "It's also because you're afraid to be thought a Jew. In Palestine you won't feel that way. Haven't you noticed the Jewish soldiers from there? I never would have believed there were Jews like that."

"You're right," said Theresa. "There's something special about them."

That night the Palestinian soldiers brought them to the mockup of the ship. Their training began. It was hard because the rope ladders they had to climb were not like wooden or metal ones. They were told to scale them in groups of ten and to descend again. Everything took place in silence, broken only by an occasional whispered order from one of their section heads which was swallowed by the sound of the waves and the chill night breeze. The sky had clouded over after a fine day, and a thin driving rain began to fall even before they left the Quonset huts. Some of the youngsters had wrapped themselves in blankets, which they threw on the sand when it was their turn to climb the ladder. Though she was draped in one, Theresa shivered from the cold. Yulek, who was sitting next to her, drew his blanket around her, and they sat there warming each other.

He could not stop thinking of that morning's conversation, of all the things he had said and all that he wished he had said. Perhaps he had taken the wrong tone. Suddenly he had a thousand other, well-phrased reasons to convince her with. He felt that since their meeting under the wet tarpaulin of the jouncing truck Theresa had begun to have second thoughts, but he couldn't help fearing that this was just his imagination. Should he have told her outright that the nuns had sold her down the river? And yet there was no denying that they had been kind to her during the war years, when she had no one else to cling to after the Jews of her town were murdered. The mother superior had been a true mother to her, and she had felt safe in the sheltering bosom of the Church. How old could she have been when brought to it? Ten or eleven, by Yulek's reckoning.

Perhaps aboard ship they would have more time to talk about themselves. He wanted to know more about her parents, her brothers and sisters, her family. He wanted to know everything about her. Robert was right, he thought, smiling to himself as he sat hanging on her every word. He was in love.

It rained and sleeted without letup for the next two days, and they left the huts only for rope-ladder practice, which continued despite the rough weather. Gradually they grew accustomed to the swaying ladders and were able to climb them quickly and in formation. If now and then someone fell to the sand below, the mishap was greeted with a gale of laughter that briefly dispelled the gray mood of the weather. Most of their time was spent on their mattresses in the huts, the boys ranged along one wall and the girls along the other, drinking watery tea and snacking on crackers and what they could scrounge from the cans. No one went to gather firewood. Not until they ran out did a few hardy souls, including Yulek, volunteeer to go for it. Yulek returned, frozen to the bone, with a huge log that he had to cut with a blunt, rusty saw. He kept looking at Theresa and sometimes caught her glance.

On the evening of the third day their section leaders gathered them and told them to get their belongings together, because the ship would soon arrive. Meanwhile they would be searched for firearms and currency, which they were not allowed to bring to Palestine.

The arms part made sense, but it was obvious that the confiscation of currency was simply a way of exacting forced "contributions" for the cause. Yulek stole a glance at Robert, who seemed to turn pale. Yulek knew that he had good reason.

After they were told to undress and stand in their underwear, the search began. As usual, no one protested. No matter how bizarre the instructions of their Palestinian leaders seemed, they were always carried out trustingly. Looking back later, Yulek decided that this was so because the group wanted to get to Palestine so badly that nothing else mattered. And maybe it also had to do with their being young, or with the fact that the more selfish ones had already left them back in Rome, some staying in Italy and others applying for visas to other countries.

Yulek had some money left from the sale of his family's house and would gladly have contributed it if asked. Why hadn't he been? The only reason he could think of was that the group leaders wished to avoid the injustice of some members of the group donating their money and others holding back theirs. He was worried about Robert, who was apt to do something irresponsible.

Yulek watched with mixed emotions as one of the searchers extracted two wads of American dollar bills from Robert's boots. It was a huge sum of money, and Yulek prayed that his best friend would not decide to walk out on them now in his resentment. Once Robert made up his mind, nothing could stop him. When it came to getting his way, he was both cunning and without any qualms.

The search lasted more than two hours. The boys stood with their backs to the girls, so as not to embarrass them when they undressed. Afterward many of the youngsters went outside, perhaps to get away from the oppressive feeling they were left with. Robert, Yulek saw, was one of the first to step out. Although he wanted to see how Theresa was, he wrapped himself in a blanket and ran after him.

The rain had stopped. Yulek caught up with his friend near the shore. The high waves made him wonder how they would ever manage to board a real ship.

He would have to keep an eye on Theresa. Robert was predictably irate.

"They had no right to do it," he said. "What do they take us for, a herd of cows they can do what they want with? That money was mine! I wanted to start a business with it in Palestine. What's wrong with that? Why do I have to live on a kibbutz if I prefer Tel Aviv?"

"But you're entering the country illegally. A kibbutz is the safest place for you."

"That's my problem," said Robert, suddenly bursting into laughter.

"What's the big joke?"

"Do I look like a sucker to you? I knew what they were going to do. I stuffed those boots with one-dollar bills and hid the big denominations somewhere else."

"How could you have known?"

"You think they're gods, those Palestinians. But they're only human. Leave it to me to find out what I want from them."

"Why didn't you tell me?"

"Why should I have? Even if I did, you would have given them all your money anyway."

Though it was the truth, Yulek felt hurt.

"Don't worry, Yulek. If you ever need money, you can always count on me. I just didn't want to have an argument with you about hiding it. You have to admit that that's what would have happened if I had let you know in advance."

Yulek admitted it. Certainly, after two wads of bills had been found in the boots of a young DP under twenty, none of the search party would have dreamed that most of his fortune was elsewhere.

"I happen to think they were right," Yulek said. "You have to understand, Robert, that they're risking their lives to bring us to Palestine. They've sacrificed weeks and months, and despite your insinuations, they haven't gotten a penny for it. The money is needed to buy equipment and to charter the ship, and we should be glad to give them all we have. I'm only sorry that I wasn't paid more for the house. And I'm not worried about what we'll find in Palestine. All I want is to get there."

"It's easy for you to talk," said Robert, shivering from the cold. He headed back for the crowded hut. "You've got Theresa."

"There's a problem with Theresa," Yulek said. "I wasn't going to tell you about it. And to be truthful, there wasn't time."

Robert stood quietly, waiting to hear more.

"Never mind," Yulek told him. They started back for the hut. When they reached it, he said, "She's not going to Palestine for the reasons that we are. She's going there to be a nun."

Robert was too startled to reply. After a while he said, "I don't believe it. Maybe that's what she's planning to do *now*. But if she cares for you, you'll make her change her mind."

"I hope so," said Yulek. Palestine, the country he had thought of all these months, would be different because of Theresa, but only if she came to the kibbutz with him. "How can I make her change her mind?" Yulek asked. "She's taken a vow."

"You don't have to do anything," said Robert. "It's enough for her to be in love with you. You're just the person to give her back her faith."

"Faith in what?"

"Stop acting so innocent," Robert said. "Why do you think I'm not going to America? Why do you think I'm still your friend even though you're such a sap? Because you give me faith too. Don't you see that?"

"But faith in what?"

"If you don't understand, don't expect me to tell you." Robert poked Yulek in the ribs. "It sounds so pompous when it's put into words. Faith in human beings, you idiot!"

"You need a girlfriend, not faith," Yulek said.

Robert laughed. "A steady girlfriend isn't for me, you ought to know that. And anyway, I'm cold and all your high ideals aren't warming me up." His teeth were chattering, but he kept talking. "Theresa hangs on to her cross and her vow because of all that she's been through. I don't think it's something you can talk to her about. She'll have to realize it on her own. Faith is the only cure for her."

"Do you think that in Palestine we'll be able to put everything we've been through behind us?" asked Yulek.

"No, I don't. Not in any deep sense. But we'll be able to forget enough to go on living. The pain will always be there, but hope will make it bearable. And

– 77 –

Theresa is full of life and love, even if she does a good job of hiding it beneath that saintly exterior."

The generator suddenly quit, and with it, the lights in the two huts. It was switched off every night at this hour to save fuel.

"It's time to catch some sleep," Yulek said. But they went on standing by the door, listening to the shriek of the wind and the crash of the waves that washed up and down the dark, desolate shore. Apart from a few pale stars peering through the clouds, there wasn't a single ray of light. A candle, or perhaps a match, flickered in a window of the hut. Far across the sea, Palestine was waiting.

7.
On Italian Roads

Melanie's journey by taxi from Rome to the villa took nearly two hours on the bad roads, though the mountainous landscape with its pretty villages made up for the arduous trip. When they reached the town at last, the first person whom they asked for directions to the villa knew exactly where it was. They drove slowly up a hill via a bumpy, winding road until they came to a castlelike building surrounded by a high wall with a locked gate. The driver honked his horn, and Melanie got out of the car. Through a peephole in the gate peered a young man, who smiled and opened the gate when Melanie spoke to him in Yiddish. Meanwhile, the Italian driver ran after her as though afraid she might abscond without paying. His broken English was not good enough for him to understand her reassurances, and only after receiving half the round-trip fare did he contentedly return to wait in the car.

Melanie found herself in a large yard. In it were several young men and women seated on stools and crates. They were peeling potatoes, and their jovial chatter brightened her mood at once. The girls gathered the peels in the laps of their aprons, the boys made piles of them on the ground, and all tossed the potatoes into a large pot of water, laughing whenever someone missed. When they caught sight of her, they stopped their work to stare. Melanie nodded hello. None of the youngsters was Julian.

"Can I help you, ma'am?" asked the young man who had opened the gate. Melanie told him that she wished to speak with the person in charge.

The young man, who was rather odd, called out, "Binyomin! Binyomin!"

An older man, accompanied by a girl, emerged from a door. Melanie inquired in Yiddish about Julian Goldenberg. No one knew a thing about him.

"A large group moved out of here just a few days ago, and we're new. Where are you coming from?"

"From Rome. I'm looking for my nephew. Do you have lists of those who were here?"

"No," said the man with a suspicious glance, wondering whether she could be a UN official who had come to question the endlessly swelling list of the villa's occupants and food requirements. "I can't invite you in," he apologized, "because the floors are being washed."

"Never mind," said Melanie. "It's a beautiful day."

"Hey-Motke," said the girl. "Go get the lady a chair."

"Julian Goldenberg is a nephew of mine and the only relative I have left from my family in Poland. That is, I *think* he's alive. I came across his photograph in this newspaper." Melanie took out the clipping and the original photo that she had been given in Jerusalem.

The girl took the clipping from her. "This is from an English newspaper," she said. "Are you from England?"

"Yes," said Melanie. "I'm an English Jew."

The girl returned the clipping, took the photograph, looked at the back of it, and asked, "Who gave you this?"

"The Jewish Agency in Jerusalem," said Melanie. "He looks so much like my brother at that age that I'm almost certain . . ."

She produced a photograph of her brother.

Motke returned with a chair. "Have a seat, ma'am," he said. Then, glancing at the photograph of Melanie's brother, Artur, he exclaimed, "Hey, that's Yulek! That's my friend Yulek!"

Melanie jumped up and retrieved the Jewish Agency photo from the girl. "Is this the same person?" she asked Motke.

"Yes," he said gleefully. "And here's Rivka and Bella."

Melanie swayed, and for a moment everything went

blank. She would have fallen had the girl not helped her sit down again.

"What did you say his name was?" asked the older man.

"Julian Goldenberg."

He exchanged a few whispered words with the girl and commanded, "Hey-Motke, go get the index cards."

Motke ran to the office and was back soon.

The older man flipped through the cards, uttering the names on them out loud. ". . . Goldenberg . . . Goldenberg Julian . . . here he is! Yes, he was here until two or three weeks ago." He glanced at Melanie's wan face and said, "Hey-Motke, go get some sugar cubes and valerian drops. They're in the medicine cabinet. And a glass of water."

"Hey-Motke this, hey-Motke that," grumbled Motke, running off.

"I'm fine, really I am," Melanie said apologetically. "I just can't believe it! Where did they go from here?"

"I don't think we can tell you that," said the girl. "You're English, after all. And it's confidential."

"But I have a letter!" Melanie showed it to them.

"Well," said the girl after studying it, "this *is* from the Jewish Agency in Jerusalem, and it does ask us to help you find your nephew. But you're English too, even if you *are* a Jew, and it's not information we can release. You'll have to . . ."

She conferred with the older man again.

Motke came running back to be told that there no longer was a need for the sugar cubes and valerian drops. In his chagrin he stuffed the sugar into his mouth and ground it loudly with his teeth. The girl burst out laughing, took the glass of water from him, and handed it to Melanie.

"I'm afraid —" began the older man.

Motke interrupted him. "They've gone to Metaponto!" he blurted out.

The man looked at him reproachfully.

"Yulek's my friend," said Motke. "I'm going to see him again in Palestine."

"Thank you very much," said Melanie with a smile.

"Well, all that's left for me to say is that I hope you find him," said the girl. "And from now on, Motke, please keep your nose out of it."

"Hey-Motke!" said Motke and began to laugh. The rest of the crowd joined him.

"We're in a very delicate situation," explained the older man, "because the English are looking everywhere for our boats and ports of embarkation. Yes, they went to Metaponto. You can take a train there from Rome. It's a little town in the south, about an hour from Taranto. You'll find their camp on the coast, a few kilometers from the town. There's no road to it, and it can be reached only by Jeep or some other all-terrain vehicle."

"But how will I find them? Here I asked for the villa. What can I ask for in Metaponto without giving you away?"

"I honestly don't know what to tell you. Perhaps for the DP camp."

"Ask for the crazy people," said Motke suddenly. "Ask for the crazy people!"

"How do you know?" asked the girl. She and the director looked equally surprised.

"Because I was there once, and they told me to wave my arms and talk to myself wherever I went," said Motke. "In the end they sent me back here because I wasn't crazy enough." Once again the potato peelers, who had put down their work to listen, joined in his laughter.

"And where are you from?" Melanie asked him curiously.

Motke shrugged. "I don't know."

"He doesn't remember anything," said the director. "We've asked him. He can't even remember his own name. He does speak Yiddish, though. I hope you've realized by now that secrecy is of the utmost importance."

"Yes," said Melanie, "I have. Your secret will be safe with me. I just wonder whether I'll be allowed to see Julian at all or even be told where he is. Do you think this letter from the Jewish Agency will help? I simply can't imagine the whole thing."

"I'll write you a note to the person in charge there," the director said unexpectedly.

He went into the building and returned a few minutes later with an envelope. "They'll believe your story," he said. "Just don't speak English to them."

"Nothing but Yiddish," Melanie promised. She rose and held out her hand. The director wished her luck and a cordial goodbye.

"*Mazel tov, mazel tov!*" chimed in Motke, and Melanie forgot her British manners for a moment and gave him a big kiss. The three of them walked her to the gate, which Motke swung wide open. The drowsing taxi driver had to be awakened. Motke stood waving by the gate. Melanie took her handkerchief from her bag and waved it back at him.

"I did it!" she said excitedly to the Italian driver, who could barely understand. "I found my nephew!"

"Bravo! Bravo!" said the driver. He pointed to the empty seat beside her and asked, "This boy, where is?"

"In Taranto," said Melanie, realizing too late that she had already said more than she should have.

"Signora want taxi Taranto?" asked the driver.

"No, no. I'll phone him from Rome and he'll come. But if I do need a taxi, I'll let you know."

"You have childs?" he asked.

"No," answered Melanie. "I don't."

"I five childs," he said proudly.

Just then the taxi veered from the road and nearly plunged into a precipice below. Melanie hung on with all her might. "Signora no be afraid. Everything okay," said the driver when the car was under control again. And as if to bolster her confidence, he began to whistle a tune from some opera. Melanie tried to identify it until she realized with a smile that the tune was two different arias mixed together.

Although it was late at night when she reached the hotel in Rome, Melanie asked the operator to place a call to London. She lay in bed with her eyes shut while waiting, dozing off and waking until the phone rang. Through the receiver came the voices of two operators, followed far away by James's.

"James, you won't believe it," she shouted into the telephone. "I've found him!"

"I can hardly hear you," said her husband. "Is he in Rome with you?"

"No. But someone identified him. He looked at the photograph and said 'That's Yulek!' And his name was on a list too: Julian Goldenberg. I can't tell you how excited and happy I am. And I miss you!"

"What are you going to do now, Melanie? Where is he?"

"I can't talk over the phone, James, do you get me? He's somewhere else, and I'm going there tomorrow. I'll keep you posted. Are you all right? Is Mary taking good care of you?"

"Everything is fine, and I'm very happy for you. I've been in touch with our embassy in Rome, and it will be at your service if you need it."

"Did you tell them why I was here?"

"No, of course not."

"I don't think I should let them know anything about it. But thanks, anyway. James, please call —"

The phone went dead.

She waited for it to come back to life, but it didn't. After a while she replaced the receiver and fell asleep at once. She dreamed about little Yulck. He was with her in the yard of their old house, and they were scattering feed for the hens.

Melanie woke early in the morning and could not go back to sleep. Rather than pace up and down in her room until it was time to take a taxi to the train station, she decided to go by streetcar. People were hurrying to work, wrapped in their coats and with collars lifted against the cold March wind. She handed the streetcar conductor some paper money — one of those funny Italian bills with lots of zeros that weren't worth much — and watched him count out her change from a wad held by a rubber band. He used a small rubber-tipped pencil to flick the bills with lightning speed while counting out loud to himself.

At the train station Melanie bought a first-class ticket and was soon deep in a thriller that she had brought to read on the trip. The ticket clerk had told her that it would be an eight-hour ride, and it was afternoon by the time they reached Metaponto.

The weather was totally different from Rome's, and not just because she had set out from the latter in the early morning. Here the sky was bright blue, and a warm sun greeted her as she stepped down onto the platform.

Although the town she had arrived in was indeed small, no one knew anything about a temporary insane asylum by the sea. No one knew where she could rent a Jeep, either. In the end a cab driver took her to a gas station, and there, using basic English, she found someone who knew where the crazy people were. The gas station attendant's son agreed to take her there in his pickup truck. He had often, he told her, sold gas for the Jeep belonging to the crazy people's guards and had once even driven it back to their camp after making repairs on it. He drove Melanie along what was little more than a goat track, following the wheel ruts and stopping when a Quonset hut loomed, with the seacoast behind it.

"No go no more, signora," he said. "You hear what say in town. Is here crazy, everyone." He touched his hand to his forehead. "Go with God, signora," he said, crossing himself.

"Wait for me here," Melanie told him.

She covered the last stretch on foot, determinedly freeing her high heels from the sand they kept sinking into, only too well aware of what her silk stockings would look like by the time she arrived.

From a distance the camp looked deserted. The sandy path ran as far as an unmanned barrier. But Melanie soon saw a second Quonset hut and several shacks among some trees. Two or three people were walking about, and farther off, on the beach, she saw someone dragging a log in the fading light. Maybe it was a woman. Two figures, those of a young man and a young woman, rose from a campfire and approached the barrier. Both looked very serious.

"*Buon giorno,*" Melanie greeted them in Italian. She then shifted to Yiddish. To her surprise, neither of them understood it. She resolved not to speak English, however, and after a while someone named Henyek was sent for.

"What kind of Jews are you that you can't speak Yiddish?" Melanie asked Henyek.

He explained to her that the Jews in Palestine spoke

Hebrew, although they knew some English. "They've also learned some Italian," he said. "I'll translate for you."

"I'm looking for someone who arrived here with a group two or three weeks ago," said Melanie, mentioning the name of the town near the villa. "I was there yesterday."

Henyek translated. The two Palestinians glanced at each other, and the younger of them said something in Hebrew.

"They left this morning, signora," Henyek translated. "You just missed them."

"Left? For where?"

Henyek translated her question.

There was no answer. The Palestinians regarded Melanie suspiciously. She handed them her two letters, one from Jerusalem and one from the villa. They read them and warmed up to her a bit.

"Look, you shouldn't have been sent here," they said. "We'll have to ask you to leave. And please try to look scared — for the driver. Your nephew sailed this morning for Palestine."

Henyek translated. Only after Melanie started back for the car, holding her shoes in her hands, did he ask the two men why they had lied to her about the ship's departure date.

"She's better off not knowing," answered the young man.

The three of them returned to their campfire.

Melanie took the night train back to Rome and arrived there in the early morning. At the hotel she placed a call to London, waking James from his sleep. The sound of train wheels hadn't stopped rattling in her head, and she still felt the swaying motion of the journey on the ancient tracks. She listened to the telephone ring and suddenly wanted more than anything to be there, at the other end of the line.

James picked up the phone.

Melanie said, "James, you sound like you're right next to me! I tell you, the telephone is the greatest invention in human history. I just got back to my hotel. I'm so disappointed. They sailed this morning. . . . Yes, just imagine! . . . No, I'm not. I'm flying back to Palestine. I have that old friend on a kibbutz whom I think I'll visit, and then I'll stay for a while in Jerusalem while I'm waiting for the ship. . . . From that man I told you about at the Jewish Agency. He'll let me know if Julian has arrived. . . . A week or two, I should think. It's a small ship and probably won't take a direct course. . . . If they are, I'll just have to go to Cyprus. . . . Has it been raining in London? I do miss you! Why don't you come? . . . You're so frightfully busy, James. I can't wait for you to retire. I'll call you tomorrow at this time. Cheerio!"

As her husband was hanging up, she remembered to shout, "James, tell Mary to take out —"

But the line had gone dead.

Melanie lay down on her bed fully clothed and thought. When she opened her eyes again, dawn was breaking. She rose, drew the curtains, hung the DO NOT DISTURB sign on the door handle, and went back to sleep.

8.
At Sea

Toward evening the *Tel Aviv* slipped out of the small harbor of Metaponto as if to depart. Soon after, it returned under cover of darkness and anchored opposite the camp, at which point the illegal immigrants were ferried to it in three dinghies. Suddenly they understood how crucial the practice runs had been, because unlike the wooden mockup, the ship did not stay still for a moment. Although Yulek was concerned about Theresa, she scrambled up the wet rope ladder and onto the heaving deck like a cat. He followed close behind her, not knowing what he might do if she were to tumble and fall.

When they were on deck at last, he asked, "Theresa, can you swim?"

"No," she said. "Can you?"

"No," said Yulek. "Who could have taught me?"

The cold on deck and the orders of their leaders drove them down to the hold. Only then did they realize what they were in for. It was not exactly how Yulek had imagined the trip to the land of his dreams. The hold was crowded and stuffy, dimly lit from above by invisible light bulbs. Some of the bunks were made of wood and some of canvas on metal frames, and they rose in tiers, with a tiny crawl space between them. While Yulek and Theresa stood debating, the top bunks were quickly grabbed, word having gotten out that they were airier and swayed less sharply when the ship rolled. In the end they took two lower bunks in which they could lie head to head. Yulek's was so narrow that he could not turn over in it and had to get out and back in again each time he wished to switch sides. He was still experimenting when, above the commotion, he heard Theresa laugh.

"You look so funny," she said, giggling.

"I can't breathe," Yulek said. "Places like these give me claustrophobia." He was shaking.

"Where's Robert?" Theresa asked.

"I have no idea," he said. "I wouldn't be surprised if by now he's wangled an invitation to the captain's cabin."

Theresa was slim enough to turn over in her bunk successfully. By now the hold was packed, and someone called out, "We're moving. Can you feel it?"

They all fell silent. It was hard to tell, because the ship had been rolling before too. And then, through the silence, came the throb of the engine, and the ship pitched harder.

"Yes," someone whispered. "We're under way."

One of the passengers began to sing "Hatikvah," the Jewish national anthem. Perhaps it was the crowding, or the darkness, or the need for secrecy that had been so impressed on them, but as more and more of them joined in the singing, they did it so quietly that it seemed like a prayer — like a plea to arrive, after so many years, on safe shores. Each was alone with his or her memories, with loved ones no longer alive.

The sea grew worse, and the days turned into one

long nightmare. Yulek and Theresa were not the first to become seasick. In the beginning they still felt well enough to go to the bathroom on deck. The guard at the top of the stairs let them out one by one and waited for each to return before sending the next. The food was the same boxes of crackers and cans they had been given in Metaponto, and even before the weather turned rough some of them relieved themselves or vomited into the empty tins and went on deck to throw these into the sea.

Theresa and Yulek slept late their first morning aboard ship and almost missed the daily distribution of drinking water. Yulek was woken for it by one of his friends from the villa and got Theresa out of bed. Otherwise there was little difference between day and night in the dimly lit hold. Conversations were rare and held in low voices. Most of the youngsters passed the time curled up in their bunks, comforting themselves that the trip wouldn't last forever. Every morning someone would announce the day, the time, and their nautical location.

Yulek and Theresa didn't speak much either. It was hard to talk with so many strangers and semistrangers lying all around them, some with eyes shut and some open. The stormier it grew, the less people could control their stomachs. Sometimes, lacking the strength or time to descend, they vomited from an upper bunk. Yulek received one such direct hit from above, although luckily he was wrapped in his blanket. He took it off and threw it under his bunk, using it afterward in place of a toilet. Theresa was sick and flat on her back.

He didn't know how to help her. In the end she had to tell him to leave her alone for a while.

The worst time of all was Thursday morning. The ship felt like it was about to break apart in the waves. Yulek did not leave Theresa's side.

"You know," she whispered through pale lips, "I just remembered something. Once when I was a little girl and had a high fever, I felt sure I was going to die. My father sat by my bed, and each time I opened my eyes, there he was. I was sure that if I opened them and he wasn't there, it would mean that I was already dead."

She finally fell asleep. Yulek remained by her side, thanking God that they hadn't managed to grab top bunks, where he couldn't have sat next to her.

Waking from a troubled sleep, he felt someone seize and grip his hand hard. It was Theresa, who had been dreaming. Without thinking he brought her hand to his lips and covered it with kisses. Then he felt badly for taking advantage of her in her sleep.

He fell back asleep himself, for how many hours or days he didn't know. Suddenly he was being shaken and a flashlight was blinding his eyes. He awoke in a fright and had to strain to remember where he was. The ship had stopped rolling. No one was retching or puking. There was nothing but silence and the throb of the engine as the ship lightly breached the water. The first thing he felt was the filthy floor beneath him.

"Yulek! It's about time I found you."

"Robert!"

"Come up on deck. Let's get out of here. How can anyone even breathe down here?"

Theresa awoke and was happy to see Robert too.

"Where have you been?" Yulek asked.

"On deck."

He couldn't believe it. "The whole trip?"

In a whisper Robert told them that he had been playing poker with the first mate and had let him win a few big hands in order to stay in his cabin. Now that the weather was better, though, everyone was coming up for air.

"What time is it?" asked Yulek.

"The middle of the night. Come. The storm's over."

"Where are we?" Theresa wanted to know.

"We've passed Rhodes," Robert said. "Come on up."

"Just a minute," said Yulek. He bent to pick up his blanket, which was full of human excrement. "I have something to throw into the ocean."

"So do I," said Theresa with embarrassment. "Go on. I'll follow you."

The two of them spent the night on deck. Robert found them a sheltered place there and brought them blankets and some water to wash up with. Then he fetched two apples, which he did not stay to share with them.

For a while Yulek and Theresa sat silently, gulping the cold, fresh sea air as if they could not get enough of it. Then Theresa said, "I don't care if I freeze to death. I'm not going down below again."

"Neither am I," Yulek agreed.

She seemed so near him, yet so far away. Suddenly he missed their bunk beds in the stuffy hold with its horrid stench and congestion. There at least he could hold Theresa's hand. But when someone tried to chase them back down there, they refused to go. Gradually they were joined by more and more people from below. The regulations were relaxed, and they were now merely required to dive under tarpaulins at the sound of a siren that signaled the sighting of a British ship or reconnaissance flight. The sailors, or someone wearing a sailor's cap, made sure that they were well covered.

It was a quiet night, one of their last at sea. The water stretched smoothly and sleepily around them, its little waves lapping at the ship and falling back in the light of a newly risen full moon. The deck was full of youngsters sitting in groups. In one of these, near Yulek and Theresa, someone began to play a mandolin. They moved closer to it, Theresa sitting with her back against a post and Yulek lying with his head propped on his elbow. Their hearts welled as they sang, feeling that the end of their long wanderings had come, and with it the promise of something that they could belong to, a home that would be theirs and for which they would be willing to give all.

The moon was so big and bright that Yulek could see every line of Theresa's face, and she turned to look at him from time to time with bright eyes. Sitting up, he confessed to her how he had kissed her hand while she slept. "And not just once," he said shamefacedly.

"Yulek," said Theresa, "I know. I wasn't sleeping."

"You weren't?"

"No."

Blissfully he took the palm of her hand and pressed it to his cheek. *She wasn't sleeping,* he kept telling himself. *She wasn't sleeping.*

When he lay down again on the deck, Theresa gently took his head and placed it in her lap. They were oblivious of Robert, who approached, glanced at them, and departed. They were oblivious of the other couples near them, some of whom were touching or embracing too. They saw nothing but the moon above the sea, felt nothing but the ship skimming the calm water. The notes of the mandolin rang in their ears, together with the singing of the group and the pounding of their own hearts.

Late at night they returned to their blankets and curled up in them to go to sleep.

Yulek couldn't fall asleep. The moon was much smaller now and far above them. Now and then footsteps crossed the deck, or a bit of laughter or quiet conversation drifted their way. From the far end of the ship came a man's voice singing an aria from an Italian opera. *It must be one of the sailors,* Yulek thought. He kept thinking of Theresa laying his head in her lap. Had the shiver he felt been her hand that did not dare stroke his hair, or was it a breeze from the sea?

He turned over to look at her. She was lying with her eyes open, staring up at the sky.

"Theresa," he said, "I love you."

"I love you too, Yulek," she said tenderly.

He had never kissed a girl before. He did it gently and bashfully, brushing her lips with his own. But when he tried to tear them away, he couldn't. Theresa began to tremble.

"What is it?" he asked.

"Yulek," she whispered in a frightened voice, "I'm so afraid."

"Of what?"

"I don't know."

He wanted to ask if it had to do with the kiss, but he didn't want to give it a name, to cheapen with a word that was bandied about so casually what had happened between them and could never happen to anyone else. No one had ever felt — no one *would* ever feel — what they had. And yet Theresa was afraid. Once again he asked her of what.

But she too did not want to give it a name.

They lay facing each other.

"Do you really think that my parents can know what's happening to me now?" Theresa asked.

Yulek remembered their conversation on the seashore in Italy. "Maybe this will seem like a silly thing to say," he said, "but no one knows what happens after death. Anything is possible. I don't think that it's just because of the vow that you wear a cross and want to become a nun."

"Does it bother you that I wear it?"

"No. It's like any other charm."

She lay there thinking about that. After a long while she said, "Then you think I'm afraid of . . ."

"Yes, I do."

"I've thought of that too." She paused for a moment.

"I think there's a fear that may never go away," she said with a quiver.

"Robert says that it will," said Yulek. "But —"

"You talked to Robert about it? I didn't think you could about things like that."

"Yes. He's full of surprises."

"Do you think that in Palestine we'll be able to forget?"

It was the exact same question that he had asked Robert.

"Robert doesn't think so," said Yulek. "Not deep down. But he says that we'll be able to forget enough to go on living. He says that the pain will always be there, but that hope can make it bearable. And faith too, he said."

"He's right," said Theresa.

They awoke to a damp, cold morning. Theresa brushed her lips against him and smiled.

"I think there must be hot tea by now," Yulek said. He rose and helped her to her feet.

In the tea line they met some of the girls from the villa. Rivka gave Theresa an unfriendly look and said, "So he's yours now, eh?"

"That's none of your business," answered Theresa, taken aback.

"Don't you worry, you little Catholic tramp," Rivka whispered in her ear. "He'll dump you when we get to Palestine."

Yulek put an end to it. "Rivka," he said, "didn't we agree not to raise that subject again until we reach the kibbutz?"

Theresa blushed. Yulek took her by the hand and went to the end of the line with her.

"I don't want to be with them in Palestine," said Theresa. "Not even for a minute!"

"There are many kibbutzim, Theresa," Yulek said. "We can ask to go to another one."

He looked at her, holding his breath. She swallowed hard and said nothing. Would she be punished for breaking her vow?

9.

Back in Jerusalem

From Lydda Airport Melanie took a taxi to Jerusalem. Recalling the unpleasant feeling she had in the heavily guarded King David, Jerusalem's fanciest hotel, she asked the driver to take her to a less touristy place and was brought to the Eden, a hotel in an all-Jewish neighborhood. After arranging her things and resting a bit, she attacked her agenda. First she walked to the Jewish Agency, where nothing had changed in the few days since she had been there. The building was surrounded by the same barbed wire and the same British soldiers, and inside, Yitzchak Fishler was sitting at the same desk. He recognized her immediately and seemed glad to see her.

"Well? Did you find him?"

"Yes and no. But I know that he's due to arrive on an illegal immigrants' ship called —"

"*Shhh.*" Fishler silenced her, looking around. "Come out into the hallway with me."

There Melanie told him briefly about her investigations in Italy.

"No such ship has arrived yet, Mrs. Faulkner."

"I know. But when it does, can you let me know? You're sure to be among the first to hear of it."

"When it arrives, you'll know. If it successfully runs the British blockade, word will get out soon enough — although not, of course, until the immigrants are safely out of sight."

He promised to call the hotel if there was news, and they parted with a handshake.

Melanie's next mission was to get in touch with Henya, her old friend who lived somewhere in the south, on a kibbutz called Shibolet, and to visit her as soon as possible. She had been told that a small ship like the one Yulek was on needed at least a week for the voyage, which according to her calculations left two or three days until its arrival. When she tried to telephone the kibbutz, however, she was unable to get through despite the operator's efforts.

She phoned Major Scott, whose secretary told her that he wouldn't be in for another two hours, and decided to send a telegram to Henya. The hotel clerk offered to do it for her.

"Is the post office far?" she asked.

"No, ma'am. It's only a quarter of an hour's walk," said the clerk. He took a piece of paper from a pad and drew her a map while explaining, "This is downtown Jerusalem. You follow this street to get to it. The British army has turned it into a fortified zone that we call Bevantown."

Melanie burst out laughing. She tried to picture the face of Foreign Minister Bevan when she told him of this at the next cocktail party.

"Perhaps I should go for you after all, ma'am," said the clerk.

"Actually," said Melanie, "I'm rather eager to see this Bevantown of yours."

The sight of it was worse than she had expected. Heading curiously up Princess Mary Street, she passed a building with high archways and entered an area crisscrossed with barbed wire and military pillboxes. Soon she came to a high fence that blocked the street, forcing her to double back and take a roundabout route to the post office on Jaffa Street. An odd feeling came over her. For the first time since the end of the war she understood that there were places in the world where new wars might begin, and that if one broke out here, she, Melanie from England, would be the enemy. It no longer felt good to be a British citizen, a subject of the mighty empire that had helped defeat Nazi Germany. Suddenly she was on the wrong side. Never before had she thought that there might be a contradiction between feeling every ounce a Jew and being proud to be British.

She sent her telegram and returned in a glum mood to the hotel. From her room she rang Major Scott again, this time successfully. At first she had mixed feelings about speaking to a man who worked for a regime that barred Jewish refugees' entry into their homeland and deported them to Cyprus. She was soon reassured, though, that he was an open-minded man with no direct connection to such measures. It was also evident that James had not just cabled him but had phoned and talked to him at length. In a jovial tone Major Scott promised her that he would not have her followed by plainclothes men, and then more seriously that he would be happy to assist her in any way he could.

It came as a relief to realize that James had mentioned to him nothing specific about the ship that Yulek was on. The major only knew that her nephew was due to arrive at some time or other with a boatload of illegal immigrants. "The problem is," he said, "that on the one hand, you'll need my help to make contact with any ship that we catch running the blockade, but on the other hand, the same help will automatically make you suspect in the eyes of the immigrants." And when Melanie said nothing, he added, "Don't you worry though, Lady Faulkner. I'm sure we'll find a solution. In the meantime it would be best for me to know where to find you if the ship turns up."

"I'm going to a kibbutz in the south tomorrow. I have an old friend there whom I haven't seen for years. I sent her a telegram. You know, I saw Bevantown on the way. Did you hear that that's what they call it?"

"Actually, it came to my attention only yesterday. I haven't sent an official report to the foreign minister yet," joked the major.

"Well, don't. I'll tell him personally."

The major laughed. "What's the name of your kibbutz?" he asked.

Melanie searched her handbag for a slip of paper. "Shibolet."

"I'd be happy to run you down there, Lady Faulkner, but it might be misinterpreted and prove embarrassing for you. You've seen for yourself how suspicious the Jews are of us British. I recommend that you take a cab. The buses reach such places only once or twice a day, and the ride is a difficult one. Of course, I won't be able to get in touch with you there, because the only telephone is likely in the main office."

Melanie tried to get a line to Shibolet again, and this time, after a long wait, she was put through to the main office. Although it took a long while to find someone who spoke Yiddish, she stuck to her decision not to speak English. In the end she was told that she would have to leave Henya a message. She repeated the content of her telegram and asked that her friend call the hotel as soon as possible.

That proved to be early the next morning. The telephone rang and it was Henya. The connection was bad, but when Melanie told her friend, who was very excited, to hang up and let her call back, Henya replied that it was too risky, because Melanie might not succeed in getting through again.

"I'm in Jerusalem!" shouted Melanie into the receiver.

"For how long?"

"I don't know. I've come to look for my nephew. He's due to arrive on a ship of illegal immigrants."

"On a what?"

"A ship of illegal immigrants."

"I want to see you."

"And I you. I'll come this afternoon."

"I'll be waiting. But how will you get here?"

"Don't worry!" shouted Melanie. "I'll manage."

"I can't hear you!" shouted Henya.

"I'll see you soon!"

"See you soon! I'm so delighted!"

They were cut off.

At Melanie's request, the hotel clerk called a taxi company and asked for a Yiddish-speaking driver. After a brief exchange, he asked Melanie to settle for one who knew German and English.

The driver was an intelligent, distinguished-looking man her age. She asked if he could also bring her back to Jerusalem.

"Today?" he wondered.

"No. I'm planning to return tomorrow."

"Of course," he said. "I'm sure the kibbutz will put me up for the night and invite me to eat in its dining room."

Melanie didn't answer. She knew nothing about local customs in this new country, but she did remember how her parents sometimes used to invite traveling Jews who were passing through their town to spend the night with them. "We Jews have to look out for each other," her father liked to say.

"How long will the trip take?" she asked the driver.

"About four hours," he said. "Plus another half-hour for a stop along the way. My car is in good condition, but the roads are not. The only thing we have to worry about is a flat tire."

Melanie soon found out that he was an ex-lawyer from Berlin who had fled from the Nazis to Palestine. She was surprised to hear that although he had been forced to give up his profession and become a cab driver he didn't regret his new life.

On the way they passed many Arab villages. Here and there they saw a Jewish one. The Arab houses were stone- or mud-colored, with flat roofs and olive groves surrounding them; the Jewish houses were white with red roof tiles that rose above orange and lemon trees. Melanie remarked that she thought the Jewish homes were much prettier. Her driver disagreed.

"The Jewish villages look like they were taken from Germany or Switzerland and put down in the wrong place," he said. "Look how well the Arab villages blend into the landscape."

"I hadn't thought of it that way," Melanie admitted. "Everyone here is always talking about how cultured and European we Jews are."

She smiled to herself at how easily the word *we* had escaped her lips. She really did feel that she belonged in this place.

"Yes, not many people think like I do," said the driver. "I have a romantic feeling for nature. Not that I'd want to raise my children in an Arab hovel."

"How many of them do you have?"

"Four. All boys."

He was warm and interesting, but although she regretted having chosen to sit in the back seat, she was afraid it would be improper to ask to move to the front at this point. Instead she leaned forward and told him about her nephew, and when they stopped at an Arab restaurant along the way, she showed him the photographs of Yulek and her brother. The resemblance, he agreed, was astonishing.

As was the custom among the Jews of Palestine, they immediately established themselves on a first-name basis. The driver's name was Meir, and he ordered two dips called *hummus* and *tahini* with fragrant green olive oil and two kinds of charcoal-grilled meat, *shashlik* and *kebab,* plus all kinds of unfamiliar salads. Melanie asked all of their names and made a mental note to tell James about them. At the meal's end they were brought a brass tray with little demitasse cups, a copper beaker of strong Turkish coffee with a long, curved spout, and small cakes filled with pistachio nuts and honey that were called *baklava.* Melanie was thoroughly entranced. When she started to ask for cream and sugar for her Turkish coffee the driver signaled her not to, explaining that such a display of ignorance would make her ridiculous in the eyes of the proprietor, who had shown her great respect. Indeed, the coffee was already sweetened and spiced; cream would only have ruined it.

They continued on their way south, the Arab hamlets getting poorer. The houses were made of mud and had thatch or rusty tin roofs. Prickly pears grew everywhere. Here and there they saw a Bedouin encampment. The few cars on the untarred concrete roads were mostly military. Now and then they passed a procession, always consisting of an Arab man riding a donkey and several women strung out behind him with bundles on their heads. Melanie was curious to know more about them, and Meir told her a bit about local Arab and Bedouin customs.

It was late afternoon when they drove through the front gate of the kibbutz, sending up clouds of dust in the yard.

10.
Kibbutz Shibolet

The workday had just ended for most of the kibbutz members, and Melanie soon found herself surrounded by kibbutzniks in their work clothes and by children of all ages. Private automobiles did not often arrive in the kibbutz — let alone transporting elegant ladies. Melanie was brought to the chicken coops, where her friend Henya worked. She found Henya sorting eggs in a little shack next to a long coop full of shrilly cackling white hens, a kerchief on her head and looking very pregnant.

For a moment Henya failed to recognize Melanie. Her eyes scrutinized the hat and the face beneath it, and only then did they light up. Both women were close to tears. Henya took off her work smock and they embraced. Although Melanie hugged her old friend hard, she did not feel a full response. Perhaps, she thought, Henya's stomach was in the way.

"You're so dressed up," Henya said, wiping invisible crumbs from her clothes. "I don't believe I've seen such a fancy hat even in Tel Aviv."

"I have a weakness for hats," Melanie apologized, feeling awkward. "This is the latest style in London."

"How did you get here?"

"By taxi."

"All the way from Jerusalem?"

"Yes. And now I've got a problem. My driver doesn't want to return to Jerusalem and come back for me again tomorrow."

"That's no problem at all," said Henya. "We'll put him up here for the night."

Henya took Melanie and Meir to the dining room. It was all so natural that Melanie ceased to worry. She looked around curiously, and Henya promised her a grand tour of the kibbutz the next morning.

The dining room was rectangular and high-ceilinged and had large windows covered with mosquito nets. In it were a dozen tables, and around each table were eight chairs. Two kibbutzniks, a man and a woman, were setting the tables for supper. Two older members were playing chess in a corner. Henya took Melanie to another corner, went off, and returned in two minutes with an aluminum kettle full of tea, two white porcelain cups, sugar, milk, and a plate of bread and jam.

"We call this kibbutz cake," she said of the bread and jam. "Supper is served at six-thirty."

"I'm really not hungry," Melanie sought to reassure her. "We had something to eat on the way."

Meir excused himself and went off to join the chess players. He instantly began a game with one of them while the other watched. All three spoke in German.

"Do you have an extra bed for him, Aryeh?" Henya asked one of the chess players.

"He needs a place to sleep? I'll find something for him. Don't worry about it."

Henya took Melanie to her room, one in a row of six that shared a common terrace. She removed her kerchief and washed her hands and face at a faucet by the door, the water from which ran into a barrel filled with gravel. "This is our shower," she apologized. Melanie looked for a bathroom but couldn't see one anywhere.

"You mean . . . there's no other place to wash up?"

"Oh, no." Henya laughed. "We have a communal shower a hundred meters from here. It has sinks and even hot water. But I prefer going there late at night, when it's empty or nearly so. You can come with me if you'd like. I'm too lazy to shower in the morning, especially in winter, so I wash and brush my teeth at this faucet."

Melanie asked about the bathroom. It was getting to be a pressing issue.

"Oh, my, you poor thing! Come, it's this way. I have no bathroom of my own. The one I use is near the shower."

They followed a paved path to the bathroom, which was cleaner, Melanie had to admit, than the average public restroom in a train or bus station. Still, she used its facilities warily. Would she have the courage to go

– 109 –

with Henya to a communal shower? Wasn't Henya embarrassed to show her big belly there? Maybe that was why she went late at night.

"Have you only one room in your flat?" Melanie asked.

"Yes. That's all anyone needs."

"Where do the children sleep?"

"In the children's house. They take their afternoon nap there too. After it they visit their parents and spend a few hours with them, and then they go back for the night."

"And you don't have your own kitchen either? Forgive me for asking all these questions, but I've never seen anyone live like this."

"My own kitchen? No, of course not. We all eat in the dining room. I think it's an ideal way to live. I'll show you around tomorrow. And Yankele will take you to the factory."

"When will he be here?"

"Any minute now. He must be showering. Couldn't you stay a day or two longer? Send your driver back by himself. We'll find a way to get you to Jerusalem."

"I'm afraid I can't. My nephew's ship should be arriving soon. I have to be in Jerusalem in case there's news of it."

Melanie told her friend the whole story and showed her the photographs.

"If the British catch them," said Henya, "they'll be deported to Cyprus."

"I know. That's why I have to hurry back. I have

a contact in Jerusalem, a British officer — Major Scott. He'll keep me posted."

"You told him about the ship?" asked Henya in a strange tone of voice.

"In a very general way."

"An English major? Don't you think that's going a little too far?"

She doesn't trust me, thought Melanie.

"Henya, I understand your suspicions. But you do know that the official in the Jewish Agency trusted me implicitly. He even gave me a letter of recommendation to Italy. And now I've been told by him that he'll put me in touch with the Jewish underground to find out where Yulek is once he arrives. Do you ever remember me acting foolishly?"

Without waiting for an answer she went on, "All I told the major is that I'm looking for a nephew who is supposed to arrive on a ship from Europe. I didn't even say where it was coming from, although he knows the ships sail from Italy. You have to realize that many people in England, not just Jews, disagree with their government's policies. I can understand Prime Minister Attlee wanting to honor his promises to the Arabs of this country, but where is his sense of fairness? What can such promises mean after what happened to the Jews in Europe? And besides, what I understand and what I feel are two different things. I'm as much a Jew as you, and my only obligations are toward my people."

Her own words surprised her. *Melanie,* she thought to herself, *you're saying something new!*

She could see that Henya felt contrite. All at once her friend hugged her warmly. It was the hug she had waited for earlier in the day, and it erased everything that had come between them since the days of their friendship in Poland, even if Henya's belly did get in the way a bit.

"Did you feel that?" Henya asked.

Melanie jumped. "What was it?"

"The baby kicked," Henya said, laughing.

"I didn't know babies could. You mean it actually . . . how exciting! I'm jealous."

They hugged again. Melanie asked, "Weren't you afraid to become pregnant at your age?"

"No. You know, after I lost my children and my husband . . . well, I just felt I had to start all over again. And the age doesn't matter so much when it's not your first birth. Even then, though, if I were you — forgive me for intruding — I wouldn't think twice about it. I'd take the risk. It's your last chance, Mela. Think of it that way."

"I wrote to you about it," said Melanie. "At first James and I wanted to be by ourselves. And then the war broke out and we waited for it to be over. And when it was, we thought we were too old to have children. Or at least that I was."

"But you're not. What are you talking about? Take my word for it. It will give your life new meaning. It's surely no accident that you of all people have been traveling all over Italy and Palestine to find your nephew, if you follow me."

Melanie felt shaken to the core, as if by something buried in her deep and long ago. How could she not have realized that she was searching for Yulek not just because he was her last living relative? She wanted a child of her own. Was it really not too late? Would James agree? Yes, if she were to insist, he would agree, despite his concern for her. And she would, she would talk to him! Henya was right. When you had looked death in the eye as Henya had, you knew how to appreciate life.

"Mela, don't be angry at me for being so suspicious of you at first. We all feel that way toward the British because of what's happening here. They keep saying they're neutral, but they're really on the side of the Arabs."

"You know," said Melanie, "I haven't been called Mela in years. I had forgotten that you called me that. It's like hearing a distant echo."

"Are you really called Melanie in England?" asked Henya.

Melanie smiled at her. Even her friends in Warsaw had never known the Jewish name that she was born and grew up with. No living person knew it except for the boy in the photograph. Overcoming her shyness, she laid a hand on her friend's stomach.

"I think I'll take your advice, Henya. I definitely will, no matter what!"

Henya's husband did not return that night. A neighbor came to tell them that he and some other kibbutzniks had gone on a mission for the Haganah, the main Jewish underground organization.

"Oh, my," said Henya. "Suppose I give birth?"

"Don't worry," said the neighbor. "I'll be here. Everything will be all right."

The neighbor's name was Betsalel, and Henya introduced him to Melanie. He was a tall, tan, strong-looking man with a bald spot. He wore a khaki shirt, khaki shorts, and sockless sandals, and he held a bundle of work clothes wrapped in a towel in one hand and a pair of muddy boots in the other. Unfortunately, he knew only Hebrew and Henya had to translate — a wearisome task.

Just then they heard a slow, rhythmic gong.

"That's to call the children to their dining room for supper," said Henya. "It's time for our supper too."

"Why isn't there a gong for the grownups?" asked Melanie.

"There is, but only for emergencies, like a fire, for instance, or trouble with the Arabs or the English. Then it's rung quickly."

The three of them set out along the paved path leading to the dining room. Melanie hesitated, then went back to Henya's room, threw her hat on the bed, and returned with only her handbag.

"You look much better now," said Henya with a laugh.

The kibbutzniks were eating and talking animatedly in the dining room, their hands conveying food and emotions at the same time. It made Melanie feel full of life and hope just to look at them. Meir the driver was there with his two new friends. *These are people,* thought Melanie, *who can do things, fight for things, achieve things!* She was happy she had come. She didn't even mind the curious looks that were sent her way from all sides.

Melanie watched the people next to her and did whatever they did. First they took the tomatoes, cucumbers, onions, and green peppers that were in the middle of the table and sliced them into a salad. Some did it patiently, dicing everything into little cubes, and some quickly and casually. Perhaps, thought Melanie — salting and peppering her own salad before pouring a bit of oil and vinegar on it — this was a way of reading a kibbutznik's character.

On the table were also plates of jam and margarine, a kettle of hot tea, and an aluminum bowl into which everyone threw the peels and leftovers. Soon a woman came by with a wagon, from which she served hot cereal, potatoes, and wedges of yellow cheese before moving on to the next table.

"For breakfast we also get half an egg," said Henya with a perfectly straight face.

"And for lunch?" asked Melanie.

"Soup, cereal, and sometimes meatballs and a vegetable. You'll see for yourself tomorrow."

Melanie decided to throw caution to the wind and go with Henya to the communal shower. She felt like an anthropologist in a new country with strange customs. It was eight o'clock when they arrived, and the shower room was empty. They undressed and hung their clothes on wall hangers above long benches. Wooden clogs lay on the wet floor, and Melanie imitated Henya and stuck her feet into a pair of them, trying not to think of whose feet had been there before hers. After slipping a few times, she quickly learned to walk in them.

They moved on to the shower stalls. The warm jet of water was invigorating after her long car trip. As they stood drying themselves, Melanie kept glancing at Henya's stomach. Except in photographs, she had never seen a nude pregnant woman before.

"Where will I sleep?" she asked.

"What do you mean, where? In our room! I'll sleep with a friend whose husband is off in Tel Aviv, and if Yankele returns in the middle of the night, he'll sleep at the neighbors'. They have a pullout bed beneath their own that he can use. He'll be the night-light. I hope he'll be back in time for you to meet him."

"So do I," said Melanie. "But what does 'being the night-light' mean?"

"That's our word for someone who sleeps in one room with another couple," Henya explained with a smile.

"Then why not let me be *your* night-light?" Melanie laughed. "I really don't want to be a bother . . . and in your condition, you shouldn't have to sleep out."

"That's out of the question," Henya answered firmly. "This is how we receive guests, and you'll have to accept it."

Melanie saw that there was no point in arguing. Once again she thought of her father saying, "We Jews have to look out for each other."

Betsalel dropped by to visit. Happily, the translated conversation with him soon ended when someone outside called for Henya. After several awkward minutes of silence, Henya returned with another kibbutznik, who introduced himself as Shlomo. He said a few words to Betsalel, who wished them a good night and left. Then, to Melanie's surprise, he turned to her in English.

"I work for the Haganah," he said. "Henya told me I could trust you."

"Definitely," Melanie said.

"We've already spoken to your driver. He's a Haganah member too. When you return to Jerusalem you'll tell the British authorities that your passport was stolen in the restaurant you ate in today. Meir will corroborate."

"But my passport is right here," said Melanie naively.

"I know it is. But we need foreign passports, especially British ones."

"But it has my name and picture on it!"

"That needn't worry you. Once it's been stolen you're no longer responsible for it."

"All right," said Melanie. With a queasy feeling she took the passport from her handbag. Although she knew she was betraying her adopted country, she tried to reassure herself with the thought that she was doing it for her real country.

"When will Yankele be back?" she asked Henya.

"I may as well tell you the truth," said Henya. "There's an illegal immigrants' ship at this very moment off the coast of Port Said in Egypt. It's evaded the British patrol boats and is due to land before dawn. Yankele went to help get the immigrants ashore. He won't be back before the morning."

"That must be Yulek's ship!" Melanie said. Henya

quickly related Melanie's story in Hebrew to Shlomo, who exchanged a few more words with her and left. Melanie was too tense even to think about sleep. How, she asked Henya, who had stayed to calm her, would she ever find her nephew once the immigrants were dispersed throughout the country? Henya promised her that it would be no problem to locate Yulek's group. Perhaps the whole shipload would be brought to Shibolet. "Everything will be fine," Henya kept saying. "Yankele will find Yulek for you. You have nothing to worry about."

Melanie calmed down, and they stayed up until late, catching up on each other's lives as though throwing a bridge over the years. Henya did most of the talking. Melanie listened, now and then wiping away a tear.

When they parted Henya promised Melanie that she would wake her if there were any developments, even if it was the middle of the night.

Henya left. Melanie stepped outside. A few street-lamps lit the paths of the kibbutz. The strong, cold wind made her shiver. She couldn't for the life of her remember where the bathroom was. Looking around and seeing no one, she went off into the bushes.

"Lady Faulkner," she scolded herself gaily, "just what do you think you are doing?"

11.
On the Beach

The last two nights of the voyage were once again spent in the crowded, airless hold. Each time the lookout spotted a distant ship or plane, the vents were covered with canvas to make the ship look like an ordinary freighter, and the feeling of asphyxiation grew worse.

From Rhodes they sailed on a southerly course toward Egypt and then veered sharply toward the Palestinian coast. According to Robert, they were due to land at a beach called Nitzanim.

"Where is that?" Yulek asked.

"Halfway between Tel Aviv and Gaza."

"What's there?" inquired Theresa anxiously.

"Nothing," said Rivka brusquely. "Yet."

After having gotten used to a bit of privacy on deck, Yulek and Theresa were surrounded by constant company again. Their eyes, when they met, yearned for the intimacy they had shared on the nights they had lain curled up in their blankets, talking in whispers and listening quietly to the throb of the engine or simply to their own breathing. Now, back in the hold, Theresa's nerves were frazzled by Rivka, and Yulek felt his old claustrophobia. Even Robert had to stay below. The final two days seemed to last longer than the first ten.

"It's like this toward the end of anything," Yulek said. And then the end came.

Like other orders they had received, the one to go on deck and prepare for landing did not seem to have been issued by anyone in particular. It simply made the rounds from person to person, group to group, bunk to bunk. *Everyone on deck — we're approaching shore!* Yulek heard the words first from Robert and passed them on to Theresa, who passed them on again while he stood repeating them over and over, first in his head, then in a whisper, and finally in such a loud voice that he had to laugh out loud.

"What's so funny?" asked Robert.

"Everyone on deck!" Yulek whooped.

"Are you all right, Yulek?" asked Theresa apprehensively. He grinned at her.

"He's fine," said Robert. "He gets this way when he's happy." And infected by Yulek's hilarity, he too shouted at the top of his lungs, "Everyone on deck!"

"Everyone on deck!" the three of them cried at once. Theresa began to laugh too.

No one joined them. The sea was rough, the ship was rolling again, and the weather did not look good.

"What time is it?" asked someone.

It was four A.M. Theresa and Yulek packed their bags and went on deck. They found a space by the railing and stood wrapped in their blankets against the cold.

"Where's Robert?"

Yulek looked for him in the first light of the dawn but couldn't see him anywhere.

"I wouldn't worry about him," said Theresa.

"I just wanted him near us," Yulek said. "In situations

like these, it's good to have someone with creative ideas."

"It's only an hour and a half to sunrise," fretted someone impatiently.

"We'll be sitting ducks in broad daylight," said someone else. "Why aren't we going ashore?"

Just then Robert appeared, holding his knapsack and mandolin and wearing his Borselino hat. Rivka, Bella, and Frieda were right behind him. Pushing their way through the crowd, they joined Yulek and Theresa at the railing.

The dark line on the horizon that blackened as the sky paled was the coast of Palestine. Despite the tension, they kept silent as told until all at once a low gasp of excitement ran down the deck and was carried off by the wind; a small light, no doubt a signal, had flickered on the coast. An order was shouted in Italian, and the anchor chain rattled down. The ship drifted for a minute, and then the anchor tugged at it and held. A rubber dinghy approached, dragging a long hawser. It made Yulek think of an umbilical cord meant to tie them from now on to the Land of Israel.

A stiff breeze was blowing. Yulek and Theresa were too excited to notice until Robert pointed out, "The wind is keeping the dinghy from tying up to us."

The words weren't out of his mouth when the dinghy capsized. This time the gasp that passed along the deck was one of apprehension. A black stain against the gray morning, the overturned boat was drifting back to shore. The hawser, however, kept moving toward them.

In the growing light they saw three heads fighting to stay above the waves.

"It's the Palestinians!" someone murmured admiringly.

"They won't be able to take us ashore in small craft as planned," Robert said. "It will take too long, and the waves are too high. It's already almost broad daylight. The English may spot us any minute."

"What happens then?" asked an older man standing behind them with his bundles.

No one knew what to answer. By now the Palestinians had reached the ship and boarded it with the help of rope ladders thrown down to them. The first frail but real connection between ship and shore had been made.

"The wind is getting stronger," someone said.

"But things are moving!" responded Yulek nervously, turning to look at Robert. Robert wasn't there.

"Where's Robert?" he asked Theresa.

Theresa didn't know either.

Some rubber dinghies were lowered from the ship, and more rope ladders were thrown down from it. The sick and the pregnant women were the first to descend, helped by several youngsters. Near Yulek and Theresa stood the ship's mascot, a ten-year-old girl who was its youngest passenger. Usually seen racing around the deck with braids flying — to the admiration of the passengers — she now stood clinging to her parents.

They all watched tensely as the first contingent struggled down the swaying ladders and into the dinghies, which thudded alarmingly against the ship's side. It seemed to take forever. The light grew brighter, revealing high waves whipped by the buffeting wind. Suddenly Yulek and Theresa saw the impossible: Robert's Borselino taking off from the bottom of a ladder and landing in a bobbing boat. It was a mystery how he had managed to talk his way into the first group.

At last the dinghies began to make for shore, propelled by their passengers, who pulled at the hawser. They were making agonizingly slow progress through the rough surf when those on deck heard a mosquito-like drone, which soon turned out to be a little airplane.

"It's the English!" cried someone.

Oh, for a magic wand to make all the passengers disappear back into the hold! The plane circled the ship.

"We've been spotted!" groaned someone despairingly.

After all they had been through, it felt worse to be caught now, so close to land, than back when far out in the open sea. Yulek and Theresa's spirits plunged. Just then there was a loud creak, and they lost their balance and fell against each other.

"They've cut the anchor," said a young man standing next to them. "They're going to try to let the waves carry us in before the English get here."

The ship lurched landward ahead of the gusting wind. As its passengers screamed and held on with all their might to the railing or to one another, the ship drove forward and grated to a stop, listing badly on one side. The waves were now very near them. They were high and fast, booming against the shore in a spray of surf.

"They'll never get us into the dinghies now," a voice said.

"We've run aground!"

"Yulek," asked Theresa, "what now?"

"Stay calm," he said. "The Palestinians know what they're doing."

Theresa believed him. "They" were indeed everywhere: on the shore, in the sea, aboard the ship, where they had mingled undetected with the passengers. These mysterious, powerful, and confidence-inspiring figures were stretched out along the hawser too, vanishing beneath the foaming waves and bobbing up again like living life buoys.

A voice suddenly gave a new order. "Everyone into the water! Grab hold of the hawser and move along to the shore!"

Pandemonium broke out on deck. "We'll all drown!" people shouted hysterically. "What about our belongings?"

"Our men are all along the rope," came the reassuring answer. "You'll all be fine."

The youngsters began to leap into the sea. The older people stood helplessly with their luggage, not knowing what to do.

"Throw your things overboard!" shouted the Palestinians. "Throw them down and we'll salvage them."

Those on board were afraid to cast their bundles and suitcases into the water. Some of these were snatched from them and thrown overboard despite their protests. "Stop clinging to all your junk!" yelled an angry voice. It was hard to tell from the deck whether the belongings floating in the water were being rescued along with the passengers. "My things!" someone screamed before the voice was muffled by the pounding surf and shrieking wind. "They're floating away! My things!"

Rivka was the first of her group to jump. She was followed by the two sisters, who urged Yulek and Theresa to leap too. Yulek hesitated. He knew Theresa couldn't swim. Next to them an older couple was quarreling. The woman refused to abandon her luggage, and the man was reasoning with her softly. Nearby the parents of the ten-year-old girl were arguing too.

"I didn't live through the war to see my daughter drown in Palestine!" wailed the woman.

"She won't drown, Shula, she won't drown! There's a human line along the whole rope."

As they screamed with fear, the girl squirmed from their grasp and plunged into the water. The two jumped after her with their belongings, which were immediately taken from them and passed along the line.

"Come on, Theresa," said Yulek, throwing off his blanket.

Only now that she let go of him did he realize how tightly she had been clutching him. He jumped first. Worse than the blow of the wave that flipped him over was the shock of the cold water, which seeped at once into his clothes and paralyzed him. Someone gripped his arms and placed them on the hawser, which he clutched while looking for Theresa. But although he wanted to wait for her, a line of people behind him was already pushing him forward. A man let go of the rope and was swept away, only to be saved at the last minute.

A Palestinian held high the girl who had jumped into the water and carried her on his back to the shore, nearly choked by her desperate grip. Following close behind him, Yulek watched with chattering teeth as the man struggled to loosen her hands from around his eyes and throat.

"How far is the shore?" yelled a voice above the din of the waves and wind.

"Just a hundred meters," came the answer.

The ground suddenly vanished beneath Yulek's feet, and he sank, together with the hawser. A second later someone fished him back up, coughing and spitting water, and his feet found the ground again. By now he had learned to hold his breath and hang on for dear life each time a new wave washed over him and to breathe and move ahead again when it had passed. He kept whispering Theresa's name to himself.

The sun rose over the coast, splitting the horizon into a bright line of sand and a darker, more distant line of trees. Someone was telling him to run across the beach and get to the tree line as fast as he could.

"The buses are waiting there. Run! Run! The English are coming!"

Yulek stood shivering. Where was Theresa? He would wait for her no matter what. There was no point in saving himself if she was caught. More and more people emerged from the water, some with knapsacks and dripping suitcases and some without. Those without ran to a pile of luggage heaped on the sand, and if they did not find their things there, raced along the beach to where the current was carrying the jetsam. Yulek ran too, his whole body convulsing. Certain that Theresa had drowned, he saw her body in every floating object.

"Theresa!" he shouted.

"Run to the buses!" the voice yelled again. "She's probably there already."

"But she was right behind me!" he called back.

By now the beach was brightly lit by the glare of the rising sun. Aground on its reef, the ship seemed very near, and the figures still struggling in the waves along the hawser looked almost life-size. No longer the cavorting apparitions they had been in the darkness, they were now advancing quickly.

"Here come the English! Get a move on!" yelled someone in Yiddish.

Yulek began to run, regaining control of his muscles. Some buses were parked near an orange grove, and he ran alongside them, looking for Theresa. But it was impossible to make out the faces inside, and there was no time. Resigned to finding her later, he boarded a bus full of soaking-wet people like himself and took a seat.

A Palestinian in blue work clothes was sitting next to him. The buses set out on a path between the trees and crossed a wooden trestle over a water channel until they came to a main road. Soon after, they reached a British roadblock. Though Yulek's heart pounded, the roadblock was unmanned, and they passed through it. On one side of them were rows of army tents and on the other some barracks.

"What is this place?" asked Yulek.

"A British army camp," said the man next to him.

"But why are we taking this route?" Yulek asked, proud to be using his Hebrew.

"Because it's the fastest way," said his neighbor. "There are buses that pass this way every morning, and we're hoping that we can get through before the British catch on."

But it was too late. Yulek's bus was the first to be stopped at the next roadblock and turned back. He didn't know which to hope for: that Theresa had gone safely ahead or that she was one of those trapped behind him.

The British took them off the buses and assembled them on large parade grounds between the barracks. From a flagpole hung the Union Jack. More and more buses drove up and were emptied out. The grounds hummed with activity. Campfires were lit, and the Palestinians among them began to switch clothes with the immigrants. At first Yulek hesitated when offered someone's dry shirt; although it was explained to him that the purpose of the exchange was to keep the British from telling the newcomers, it didn't seem fair to trade his dirty, wet shirt for a dry one. He was still debating with himself when someone else came along and snatched the dry shirt from under his nose.

Yulek wandered from fire to fire in a desperate search for Theresa. He couldn't find her anywhere. Even his happiness at running into Rivka was short-lived, since he turned pale when she asked teasingly, "Where's Theresa? Don't tell me she's drowned!"

Quickly she reassured him that no one had drowned

and that Theresa must have been on one of the lead buses that passed the roadblock unhindered.

Surrounded by a host of young immigrants, a group of Palestinians was sitting in the middle of the parade grounds, giving orders. The first of these was for the Palestinians to burn their IDs. These they threw into the campfires, around which they and the immigrants had begun to dance, partly to warm themselves and partly to keep up their spirits.

Yulek joined a circle. He had always been a good dancer. Now, in this whirling Palestinian hora, he felt linked to everyone by an electric current that passed through them all despite the many different places they had come from and the different languages they spoke. They had become a single body, and he felt proud to be a part of it. With his arms around the shoulders of those next to him, he wondered what the English soldiers must be thinking of the wet, tired refugees who should have been slumped in discouragement, awaiting their fate. The thought made him dance and sing even more fervently.

"Who are *we?*" called the hora leader to the rhythm of the dance.

"Yisra*el!*" came the answer in unison: the People of Israel.

It seemed to go on forever. Yulek's heart was overflowing. Could the phlegmatic English soldiers understand what they were watching? What sense could they make of these kibbutzniks who were ready to risk deportation themselves in order to prevent it from being inflicted on a group of illegal immigrants they had never seen before? And what did it matter whether it made sense to the British or not?

In the end the group was lined up for processing. The soldiers placed them in rows and made them pass one by one between two railings formed by metal pipes, until they reached a British officer who tried to separate the immigrants from the Palestinians. He carefully checked the insides of their shirt collars — according to one theory, to see whose clothes were wet from the sea, and according to another, to look for the kibbutz's laundry mark — but it was a hopeless task. They had swapped shirts long ago, and their only answer to any question asked was, "I am a Jew from the Land of Israel."

After a while the selection stopped, and they all sat or sprawled out on the parade grounds to wait. Yulek was with Rivka and the two sisters. Little by little they were joined by others from the villa. By now their clothes had dried, but it was nearly midday and they were hungry.

"They're trying to starve us," said someone.

"How can they be so cruel?" asked Rivka. "After living through the war and getting here in one piece, you'd think we deserved a better fate than this!"

Eventually some British plainclothes men arrived, and the selection process began all over again. Once more they were lined up by the hundreds, and once more there was no telling who was who, especially because after so many hours of not eating and drinking the kibbutzniks looked as pale and wan as the refugees.

"I'm a Jew from the Land of Israel," declared Yulek each time he was asked to identify himself.

The hours slipped by.

"They're trying to break us," someone said.

In the afternoon they were served tea with milk and crackers like the ones they had eaten aboard the ship. From time to time Yulek rose and wandered restlessly to look for Robert and Theresa, even though by now he was sure that they had gotten through the roadblock. On one of these rounds, he spied the kibbutznik who had sat beside him on the bus. He was talking to a pale young man, and Yulek approached to ask what kibbutz he was from.

"Shibolet" was the answer.

12.

The Meeting

Although Melanie had been told before going to sleep that the room had no heat because "it never gets cold here," the chill woke her in the middle of the night. Full of admiration for people who could live like that, she rose and found two more thin blankets, put socks on her feet, and went back to sleep, until she was woken by Henya calling to her from the doorway.

"Henya? What is it?" All at once it came back to her

where she was, and she sat up excitedly in bed. "Have they landed?"

"They have. And they're being brought to Shibolet. Come right away to the dining room."

"I'm coming."

Melanie dressed quickly, debated for a moment, and left her hat and handbag in the room. A moment later she thought better of it, stuck the handbag under the mattress, and raced to the dining room. How, she wondered, could people live without locks on their doors?

The illegal immigrants were wet and tired but in an exuberant mood. They looked around with eager eyes, taking everything in. Many had bundles and knapsacks that were wet too. Henya and the other kibbutzniks served them tea and "cake." Melanie scrutinized their faces. The boy from the photograph was not there. Nor did anyone know anything about him.

"Is this the whole group?" she asked with disappointment.

"Not at all," said Henya. "These are just the first two busloads. There are hundreds more immigrants still to come — I've been told that the ship had eight hundred passengers. They had to be brought ashore as quickly as possible when it ran aground and was discovered by the British."

A photographer arrived, positioned his heavy camera on a tripod, draped a black cloak over it, and began to photograph the newcomers for the forged IDs they would be issued.

Melanie asked to help and was given a job by Henya.

So was Meir the driver, who had arrived in the dining room too.

Meanwhile another busload of immigrants arrived, and Melanie resumed searching for her nephew. She found an unusual young man wearing a sporty hat and carrying a dry suitcase, backpack, and musical instrument wrapped in a blanket. With him was a soaking-wet girl to whom he attended devotedly, screening her with a blanket while she changed her wet clothes and wrapping her in it as she gripped a glass of steaming tea with shaking hands. They spoke in Polish. Melanie asked them if they knew Julian Goldenberg. The girl gave a start, spilling tea on the table.

"You know him?"

"Yulek Goldenberg is a good friend of ours," said the young man. "He should be here soon. I hope so, anyway. Why are you asking about him? He never mentioned knowing anyone in this country."

"I live in London," explained Melanie. "Wait, I'll be right back."

She ran to Henya and Yankele's room and returned out of breath with Yulek's photograph. They identified him at once.

"Yulek once told me about an aunt of his in London," said the girl. "Is that you?"

"Yes, it is. My name is Melanie."

"He said he had an Aunt Malka," said the girl awkwardly.

"That's right, my dear. My name was Malka. What's yours?"

"Theresa. I'm a friend of Yulek's. I'm so worried . . ."

She tried drinking from her empty glass.

"You'll see, he'll be here soon," said the young man. "You spilled all your tea."

Theresa mechanically handed him her glass, and he refilled it.

"Are you Yulek's girlfriend?" asked Melanie.

"Yes," said Theresa, her teeth chattering.

Melanie couldn't resist stroking the girl's wet hair.

"I'm Robert," said the young man. "I'm pleased to meet you. Yulek and I know each other from the concentration camp."

Melanie shook his hand.

"How did you know that Yulek was on this ship?"

While Melanie told them about coming across her nephew's tracks but always being a step behind him, she kept spreading jam on slices of bread for Theresa, who stopped eating after the second slice. Robert, however, had a healthy appetite. Their turn came to be photographed, and an hour later they were handed papers that read "Government of Palestine." When Theresa was asked to choose a Hebrew name for herself, she refused.

"At least take a Hebrew first name," urged Shlomo, the kibbutznik to whom Melanie had given her passport. "You're beginning a new life. The past is over."

"I want my old name," Theresa protested.

"How about Tirtza?" suggested Shlomo.

"Tirtza?" Theresa grudgingly agreed to it. At least it resembled her Polish name.

"What shall I put down as your place of residence?"

"I'd like to request that she stay here in Shibolet," put in Melanie, and Shlomo accepted the suggestion.

Robert was given the choice of Rami or Re'uven and picked the latter. He declined to change his family name.

"Residence?"

"Tel Aviv."

"What is that supposed to mean?" asked the surprised Shlomo.

"Tel Aviv. You know — the city," said Robert.

"We can't give you papers that say Tel Aviv. You have to belong to one of the kibbutzim in this area. Besides which, if you were living in Tel Aviv, you'd have a street and house number too."

"All right," said Robert. "Put me down for Shibolet."

"Does that mean you'll live here?"

"No."

Shlomo hesitated.

At first Melanie did not understand what was happening, but as soon as it was explained to her she took Robert's side. Perhaps, she thought, she was asking too much in return for the favor she had done Shlomo, but in the end he agreed to this too. Robert had told her that he had a friend in Tel Aviv and all kinds of plans. Indeed, when he found out that Melanie had reached the kibbutz in a taxi, he asked if she could give him a lift on her way back.

"But I'm going to Jerusalem," she said.

"That's fine," said Robert. "From there I can get to Tel Aviv. This place gives me the feeling that you can't get anywhere from it."

"I'll be glad to take you," said Melanie. "I'll even put you up for the night in a room in my hotel."

Before long, word got out that the English had rounded up all the other immigrants. Theresa's concern for Yulek grew, and Henya began to worry about her husband. By now it was time for Henya to go to work in the chicken coops, but before she joined her there Melanie wanted to accompany Theresa to her new quarters. While Robert kept an eye on the taxi, which was his ticket to the future, she and Theresa followed a kibbutz member to a cluster of white tents. Like a lifelong kibbutznik, Melanie found the faucet with its drainage barrel at once and began to explain its uses to Theresa. The "bathroom," though, was a surprise to her too. It was a white shack consisting of two narrow cells, each with a tin roof and a rectangular concrete floor that had a round hole in the middle. As nonplussed as she was, Theresa stepped inside, locking the door behind her. When she emerged she said lightly, "Saves you the bother of flushing."

"What are Yulek's plans?" asked Melanie as Theresa hung her wet things on a wash line in front of her tent.

"He wants to live on a kibbutz. He believes in the way of life. He used to argue about it with other members of our group in the villa in Italy."

"And you?"

"I'd like to talk to you about that, Mrs. Faulkner."

"Theresa, you can call me Melanie."

Theresa's tent mates arrived and began arranging their things, and Melanie suggested that they go for a walk. She waited patiently while they strolled for a while in silence.

"Are you a Christian?" asked Theresa at last in an emotion-fraught voice.

"I never was baptized, if that's what you mean. I see Yulek knows more about me than I thought. I was under the impression that all the children in the family were told that I went to London and died there."

"He said that his father told him the truth about you before dying in the concentration camp."

"So Artur is dead . . ." Melanie mused. "You asked if I'm a Christian. Well, our friends are mostly Protestants, and I observe the same customs they do. But I also light candles on the Jewish Sabbath and go with my husband to friends' house for the Passover Seder. He even wears a skullcap and is very proud of himself."

"Forgive me for asking but . . . do you have children?"

"Unfortunately, no. Maybe . . ." Melanie smiled to herself, remembering the previous day's resolution.

"What would they be if you did?"

"I have no idea."

They fell silent. The signs of Theresa's inner conflict were visible on her face. She began to speak, checked herself, and then burst out, "During the war I was hidden in a convent and became a Catholic because I loved the mother superior. I also took a vow to become a nun if I was saved. That was after I found out that my whole family had been killed. Now I don't know anymore."

Melanie listened. This was her second encounter in the last twenty-four hours with a survivor of the Nazi Holocaust. It suddenly struck her that each one of the hundreds of illegal immigrants now being detained by the British had a similar story — Yulek too. For the first time, the Hitler years — which she had often talked about with her husband and British officials in London — seemed painfully, unacceptably real to her. She felt suddenly glad that she had given her passport to the Jewish underground.

"Have you told anyone about this?" she asked.

"Only Yulek," said Theresa.

"And what did he say?"

"Not to talk about it. To let it seem as if it had never happened."

"That's good advice. I'm so sorry he's not a little boy." Theresa didn't follow her.

"If he were, I'd take him back to London with me," explained Melanie. "I'd even do it if he were a bit older. I was seventeen myself when . . . But tell me a little about yourself, Theresa."

Theresa's face lit up. She told Melanie how she and Yulek had met, how it had finally dawned on her that she would never be a nun in Palestine, how she was growing angrier and angrier at the thought that the nuns had traded her for a shipment of food and money. No matter how she tried to justify it, she felt wounded to the quick. It was like losing her family all over again.

Melanie had only to think of her own life to understand what such a sensitive, beautiful young girl must be feeling. She sat down with Theresa beneath a spreading acacia tree, on a bench beside the lawn that fronted the dining hall. There she began to tell Theresa about herself, starting with her childhood in a small Polish town in which many of the houses still had farmyards. She told Theresa how she had met James and fallen in love with him, and about the enchanted evening when, beneath an umbrella, he turned to her, gently took her chin with his fingers, and kissed her for the first time.

"You mean that for you too it was . . ."

"It was and it wasn't." Melanie laughed. "I was already thirty, and I had some married friends. I had read lots of books on the subject, but I was still afraid at first. There are things you're taught when you're little that never leave you."

She fell silent for a moment and put her arm around Theresa, who was sitting very close to her. Like a child to her mother, Theresa snuggled up to her. *It's so natural,* thought Melanie. Although she would soon be far away again in London, she would always feel near these suddenly discovered children.

They sat there for a long while. Theresa told Melanie about Yulek and his trip to Poland, when he sold his family's house to the strangers who were living in it.

"I knew they were lying!" exclaimed Melanie angrily.

Henya returned from work, and she and Melanie went to eat lunch together. While they were there two more small groups from the ship reached the dining room, the second consisting of detainees released by the English, who were doing everything they could to identify the illegals.

"What about Yankele?" Henya asked one of those released.

"Well, one of us had to milk the cows. We flipped a coin. Yankele stayed behind to help organize things."

"But suppose he's deported to Cyprus?"

"They won't keep him there for long. He's too old," said the man with a laugh.

"But I'm due to give birth any day!" exclaimed Henya when he was gone. "I want Yankele here."

"Then why didn't he come to milk the cows?" asked Melanie.

"Because the other man's wife is pregnant too." Henya sighed.

They finished eating in silence. Henya had to go back to work. Her condition forced her to waddle like a duck, which made Melanie feel sorry for her. Back in the main office, she asked to place a call to Jerusalem. The man in charge did his best, patiently cranking the handle of the old-fashioned telephone in an effort to get the operator. In the end Melanie was put through to the office of Major Scott, but his secretary didn't know when he would be in. She returned to the dining room to consult with Shlomo, who didn't believe that she would be permitted to see the immigrants in the army camp, even if she had her British passport. Still, he said, handing the passport back to her, there was no harm in trying. Melanie promised to return it that very day.

She set out in the taxi and showed her passport to the guards at the roadblock, who let her through. After asking Meir to drop her off by the gate, she flashed it again to the sentries and was ushered by a soldier to an office. Although startled to see an Englishwoman at his door, the officer inside refused to give her permission to see the detainees. He was polite but firm, and nothing that she said could make him change his mind. In the end it was he who changed her mind by asking, "Do you intend to take your nephew back to London?"

"No," said Melanie. "I want him to stay in Palestine. It's what he wants and has fought for."

"In that case, Lady Faulkner," said the officer with a grin, "I suggest you let events take their course, because if you identify him now, we'll have to deport him. Once he's out of our hands, I'm sure that your husband and Major Scott will be able to use their influence on his behalf."

"But I want to see him. I only want a look at him!"

"I can promise you that he won't look the way he does in the photograph. They're all terribly unkempt and unshaven and wearing the oddest assortment of clothes. That's what makes it so hard to know who's who. It's like in the famous story by Kipling. But I don't suppose you've ever heard of him."

He was so surprised when Melanie knew who Kipling was despite her marked Polish accent that he reversed himself on the spot and escorted her to a shack near the parade grounds. Hundreds of people were sprawled there, some sitting and others lying slumped against their bags, surrounded by barbed wire and sentries. A few campfires were still burning, and here and there a wet shirt or piece of luggage was drying. Melanie tried to open the window of the shack. It was stuck, and the officer had to help her. Before she knew what she was doing she put her head through it and called out at the top of her voice, "Yulek! Yulek! Yulek!"

Most of those on the parade grounds were too far

away to hear, but the ones who were nearer looked up at her. The officer gently took her arm, then released it when he felt her resist.

"I'm looking for Yulek Goldenberg!" Melanie went on shouting in Yiddish. "I'm his aunt Malka. Is there anyone out there by that name?"

Now the sentries glanced at her too. The officer took her arm again, led her away from the window, and locked it. Melanie apologized. She had not, she explained, meant to shout like that but had done it on the spur of the moment. "I do hope I haven't got you into trouble with the camp commander," she said as the officer walked her to the taxi.

"I *am* the camp commander, madam," he replied, accepting her apology. "You have to realize that we lost two of our men this morning. They drowned trying to arrest some of the immigrants who were still aboard ship. It was a very rough sea. You have my word for it, however, that none of the detainees has been harmed."

"But I was told that your men opened fire," Melanie said.

"So they did. They were ordered to fire at the ground to turn back immigrants trying to escape. I must tell you that although I am obliged to carry out government policy I have the highest respect for these people. I admire them and their powers of endurance, the kibbutzniks and the immigrants equally."

They parted with a handshake. "Will the immigrants remain here long?" Melanie asked.

"I haven't received instructions yet," said the officer. "Not that I could tell you more even if I had."

Melanie returned to the kibbutz and went to the chicken coops to say goodbye to Henya. Henya promised to look after Theresa, whom Melanie found in her tent.

"I'm off to Jerusalem," she said to her. "I have a friend there, a British major, who should be able to help us find Yulek."

"Will he be able to free him too?"

"I hope so. I promise to do my best, Theresa."

Theresa threw her arms around Melanie and kissed her warmly.

Meir the driver was waiting in the taxi, and Robert was sitting in the back. Melanie asked him to move to the front and took his place. Only then did she realize how tired she was.

13.

Heading Back

As darkness fell, the British brought the immigrants some canned food and canisters of weak coffee, and they all sat down to eat. Shortly after, they heard the roar of many vehicles drawing up in a long line on the road. Yulek counted twenty-five canvas-topped trucks. On each stood two soldiers, one by the tailgate with a Tommy gun and the other with a Bren machine gun that rested on the cabin roof.

They all climbed aboard with their things. The soldiers fastened the tarpaulins, and they set out in a convoy. An hour passed and then two, and still they traveled. One of the Palestinians managed to loosen the canvas at the back, looked out, and said they were traveling eastward.

"To Transjordan?" someone asked.

"I think they're trying to take a detour around the Jewish areas to prevent riots, but in the end we're probably headed for the port of Haifa and deportation to Cyprus. Your ship did better than most. It was one of the few that's managed to get past the blockade at all."

Yulek made his way to the back of the truck and peered out at the landscape. The moon lit the trees by the roadside and the bare hills, in which a small light shone here and there. Only then did it sink in that he was really in the Land of Israel. They could deport him if they wished, but meanwhile he was there, in his homeland. There was no taking that away from him.

"Beit-Nabala," said a Palestinian, pointing at some houses along the road.

The man who had said they were being driven to Haifa declared, "They'll take us via Latrun to Jenin and from there to Faradis and Haifa. It's the most logical route."

Yulek sat between the two sisters and Rivka, on one of whose laps he dozed off. He dreamed of Theresa tossing on the high waves between the listing ship and the shore. Although he wanted to jump into the sea to save her, Rivka grabbed hold of him and stopped him. He began to yell and woke to find someone shaking him. At first, before the roar of the truck reminded him where he was, he thought he was aboard the ship. Then he fell asleep again.

A sharp jolt roused him. The truck had come to a halt. It was beginning to get light out.

"What time is it?" asked Yulek.

Someone said that it was past four. "A.M. Did you have a good snooze?"

"Yes. But where are we?"

"In the port," said a man with a familiar voice.

"What port?"

"Haifa," answered Rivka. It was on her lap that Yulek had slept.

He sat up, fully awake now.

The soldiers undid the canvas top, letting in a cool breeze. Yulek licked his lips, tasting the salty sea air. Over a loudspeaker came the order: "Out of the lorries! Everyone out of the lorries!"

The order was given first in English and then in an English-accented Hebrew and was greeted by a chorus of boos. No one got out. Then a familiar-sounding voice called out, "Stay in the trucks! Put up passive resistance! Put up passive resistance! This is an order to all of ya!"

Although everyone had heard them, the words "passive resistance" were passed again from person to person.

They all lay down on the floors of the trucks and held on to whatever and whomever they could. The British soldiers dragged them to their feet one by one and shoved them to the ground below. Anyone who resisted was prodded by a bayonet in his backside. Yulek felt a sharp poke in his rear and jumped down to a quay beside some railroad tracks. Dirt and mud were everywhere.

Shouts and screams came from the other trucks, where the soldiers were using clubs and rifle butts and dragging the occupants out by the hair. Despite his sore rear end, Yulek decided that he preferred bayonets. It was an eerie scene against the backdrop of the gray dawn, with Mount Carmel rising against the sky behind the pale lights of the port. Cranes, visible through the rapidly lifting mist, hovered over a waiting ship. It was a large freighter with a high fence on its deck, the kind that screens off a tennis court.

"It's been specially fitted for deportations," said a Palestinian behind Yulek. "We ought to be blowing the damn thing up."

"It looks so much bigger than the ship we came on," said Yulek.

"It's called the *Empire Royal*," the Palestinian told him. "It's a ten thousand tonner."

The trucks stood in a long line between rows of barbed wire. Forced to descend, their passengers lay or sat on the ground. Large numbers of British soldiers circulated among them, while others stood guard behind the wire. Yulek stretched out on the quay, his head cradled in his arms, feeling cold but grateful that Theresa was safely elsewhere.

For himself, he felt a comforting pity at being expelled from the land he had longed for so deeply and been in for so short a time. The British would not get away with it. He would return. And not only because of Theresa.

The British soldiers split into teams of five or six and began moving the deportees past the coils of barbed wire and up the ramp of the ship. Some were carried by their hands and feet; those who weighed more were dragged along the filthy quay and up the ramp. It took a long time, because there were even more Jews than soldiers. Yulek tried to calculate their numbers as he lay waiting for his turn. There had been about forty passengers in his truck, and since he had counted twenty-five trucks, there were about a thousand people. Some of the immigrants had made it past the British roadblock, which meant that hundreds of Palestinians were among them. It was amazing, the thought of so many people not only leaving their homes and families for an indefinite period and no compensation, but doing so with such enthusiasm and commitment.

The soldiers were losing their patience and grabbing bodies by whatever part of them they could. Yulek watched a young woman being dragged by her legs while her head banged against each rung of the ramp. Some of the deportees began to fight back. Here and there a soldier struck someone with a rifle butt. The atmosphere was charged. Voices called out:

"Gestapo!"

"Nazis!"

"S.S.!"

An older, dignified-looking man was saying something to the British soldiers in English. Although Yulek did not know what the words meant, they were obviously a reproach. Some of the soldiers stared at the ground. Others advanced on the deportees with redoubled fury.

Several soldiers were trying to lift Rivka, who struggled to resist. One grabbed her hair and pulled while she screamed with pain. The more slender Bella and Frieda were carried up the ramp. So was Yulek, who was tall but thin. He wondered whether he could have remained so limp if he had seen Theresa being dragged the way Rivka was. Once more he felt thankful that Theresa was not there. For a moment he grinned at the memory of seeing Rivka manhandled, but then he felt contrite. He would find her and stay by her side on the voyage to Cyprus. Perhaps she would need his help.

A British plainclothes man stood on deck trying to screen out the Palestinians. Either he had a magical sixth sense or the British were resolved to take no more people to Cyprus than had come on the refugee ship, even if they had to guess who was who. Many of the deportees were returned to the quay, some for reasons that Yulek could not fathom and some because they had been injured in the struggle with the British. For a moment he felt a flicker of hope. But now he was made to pay for his refusal to exchange shirts on the parade grounds, since the plainclothes man looked at his dirty collar and waved him on.

Of the three hundred people taken back off the boat, no more than one hundred were Palestinians. It was really impossible to tell them apart. Yulek was handed a blanket and a heavy metal mess kit and made to descend a ladder to the hold. A tapping sound on the bulkhead of the bare compartment was a sign that another, similar space was occupied too. Soon the Palestinians on both sides began to communicate by Morse code. Yulek did not see Rivka or the two sisters, who were either in the next compartment or back on shore.

It was afternoon when the engines started up. The ship vibrated while the propeller began to turn and the rattling anchor was lifted by its winch. As they pulled out of the harbor, their arrival in Palestine twenty-four hours earlier already seemed to Yulek like a distant dream. Before him flashed a picture of the immigrants jumping into the sea, their belongings clutched in their hands. The Palestinians hadn't understood why anyone would risk his life to hang on to these miserable bags and bundles — "all that junk," as they called it. Perhaps this was because they belonged to kibbutzim, where there was no private property, and perhaps too because it failed to occur to them that the newcomers, who clung to their luggage as to their own selves, had nothing else left from the past.

In the middle of their compartment a vent led down to a second hold beneath them, the ladder to which had been removed. Tired and dirty, the immigrants spread their blankets on the floor and lay down. After a while British army rations, including the familiar hardtack, were lowered to them in tin containers.

Once the ship was at sea they were permitted to leave the hold in groups of five or ten for the purpose of going to the bathroom or fetching drinking water. Soon the first groups returned with word that they were heading not for Cyprus but southward along the coast, escorted by two destroyers. No one knew what to make of it. When they were passing Tel Aviv it was Yulek's turn to go on deck. He first went to relieve himself and then turned to gaze at the Jewish city with its white houses that were picturesquely framed by the mosques and church towers of Arab Jaffa. Then, while a nearby soldier let him go on looking, his glance shifted to the two destroyers with their frighteningly bristling guns.

Just then the ship cut its engines, and Yulek heard the anchor being dropped. What now? The soldier ordered him below deck before he had a chance to find out.

There was nothing to do but wait. No one understood what was happening. They were in the middle of dividing the rations when suddenly the whole ship shook and seemed to lurch into the air. Yulek lost his balance and grabbed at the bulkhead to keep from falling.

"What was that?" yelled somebody in alarm.

"The Palestinians have blown up the ship!" someone else shouted happily. "Now we can't be deported!"

A minute later there was a dim, muffled boom. From the neighboring compartment came the message in Morse code: A D-E-P-T-H C-H-A-R-G-E.

For the next two hours the *Empire Royal* and its escorts remained facing Tel Aviv while additional depth charges were dropped, apparently in an attempt to keep Palestinian frogmen from damaging the ship even more. But in the end the immigrants' high hopes proved false, for the ship set out again, and reports came from the deck that it was now on a northwesterly course and had left the coast behind. Vats of hot soup, tasting wonderful after the long, hard day, were lowered to them by the soldiers. Soon, though, the going grew rough, and Yulek felt seasick and threw up before he could reach the deck. He wasn't the only one. The voyage quickly turned into a nightmare, the only comfort being the knowledge that it would be short. Yulek lay on his blanket in a corner beneath the dim, flickering bulbs that lit the hold. On the pretext of going to the bathroom, he managed to make three trips to the deck for a breath of fresh air. The moon, no longer full, peeked out now and then from its cover of clouds and made him long so terribly for Theresa that he preferred to go back down to the dark, airless hold and bury himself in his blanket.

14.

A Fighting Spirit and Fresh Disappointment

Major Scott was on hand to greet Melanie in the lobby of the Eden Hotel in Jerusalem. Despite the bumpy road and the loud arguments between Meir and Robert, she had slept through most of the trip back from the kibbutz.

"Zionism," Meir had answered when she asked what they were quarreling about.

Melanie excused herself for a moment while she went to book a room for Robert. He declined the money she offered him for his next day's trip to Tel Aviv and even insisted on paying his own hotel bill. Now it was Melanie's turn to refuse.

"Believe me," she said, "I have a lot more money than you do. I have no idea what you're planning to do with yours, but you'll need every cent of it."

Robert thanked her and went to his room, and Melanie sat down to talk with Major Scott.

"We have to get to Haifa," said the major. "I've booked a room for you there at the Hotel Zion. It's a perfectly decent place. I would have preferred the Hotel Carmel, but I thought you'd rather be down by the port."

"Are they already being shipped out?"

Major Scott told her that an order had arrived from London to transfer the entire group of illegal immigrants and Palestinians to Haifa; to try once more to separate them there; and to send the remaining group to Cyprus on the *Empire Royal*. Eventually the Palestinians in the group would give up their game, confess who they were, and be allowed to return. At that very moment a convoy of buses was taking a roundabout route to Haifa under heavy armed protection and would reach the port in the morning.

"All right, let's go," Melanie decided. "I'll pack a few things and wash up. Shall I order a taxi?"

"No, I'll take you myself. It's all been seen to."

"I'll find my nephew when they're loaded onto the boat!"

"It's not so simple," said Major Scott.

He explained to Melanie that there might be resistance and that no one knew exactly what would happen at the port, the military commander of which had at first refused to grant her entry to it.

"I had no choice but to tell him the truth about you," said the major. "Otherwise he would never have allowed it. The problem is that my contacts are with senior officers, who have to go by the book. It could cost them a promotion if they didn't. A junior officer might be persuaded to let your nephew slip away, but I don't know any."

"This entire policy of yours is a scandal," said Melanie angrily. "I have no words strong enough for it."

"I agree. But orders are orders."

"Then why the rush to get to Haifa?"

"There is always one last selection as the ship is boarded, and some of the illegals are then able to pass themselves off as locals and get sent to a kibbutz. The CO has agreed to let you inspect every vehicle leaving the port and has promised to turn a blind eye if you find your nephew in one of them. If you don't, you'll know for sure that he's on his way to Cyprus."

Melanie could not resist telling the major that she had already gotten a glimpse of the detainees at the army camp in the south. "They couldn't tell them apart there either," she said.

"I know," replied Major Scott. "It's terribly hard, especially since many of the kibbutzniks themselves are recent arrivals and don't speak good Hebrew yet. And of course, they've all burned their papers."

Melanie wrote a note to Robert, packed her suitcase, and set out with Major Scott for Haifa.

By seven A.M. the two of them were at the gate of the port, from which large numbers of troops could be seen everywhere. After about four hours, the first groups of those released began leaving the port. Even though they were unwashed and grimy and some had injuries and bruises, Melanie was confident of recognizing her nephew at once. But he was not among those who passed through the gate.

Melanie remained there with Major Scott until the *Empire Royal* sailed.

"What do we do now?" she asked.

"That's up to you, Lady Faulkner," said the major.

"What will happen when they reach Cyprus? Another selection?"

Major Scott burst out laughing. "I'm sure of it. Our best estimate is that at least a third of the deportees are Palestinians. In the end most of them will come forward and present themselves. The problem is that the detention camp authorities in Cyprus don't want to let a single Palestinian in, because they're known to be trouble-makers."

"But if most of the Palestinians will own up in the end anyway, why didn't they already do so here?"

"To allow as many illegal immigrants as possible to

be let back in instead of them. Once the illegals have been released by us, they can't be deported anymore."

"Can you arrange for me to be present at the selection in Cyprus?"

"I can try."

"The boy doesn't know that I'm here. I want to see him. If he fails the selection again and remains in Cyprus, I want to be able to get in touch with him. And there's something else that I have to do for him now too."

"I still have five days of leave left," said Major Scott, "and I'll gladly put them at your disposal."

"I'm terribly sorry to make you spend your holiday like this. If I had known . . ."

"Don't even mention it. Five days are all I have, but I'm only too happy to dedicate them to Lady Faulkner."

Melanie told her husband's friend about Theresa.

"It's no longer just a matter of my wanting to see him, Major. I simply have to get him out of there and bring the two of them together again. And you have to help me. Can't the high commissioner of Palestine give Yulek a special visa?"

"Of course he can. Such visas don't count as part of the general Jewish quota. But if that happens, the boy will arouse the suspicion of the Jewish underground organizations. They'll think he's a British spy or operative, and that's dangerous. Some of the more extreme underground types wouldn't think twice about putting a bullet in him. They hate our guts. Think of the King David Hotel blast."

"Well," said Melanie, "while I wouldn't justify it, they have good reasons for hating you."

"For hating *you*. Aren't you also a British subject, Lady Faulkner?"

"I am. But I'm so ashamed of British policies in Palestine that I had forgotten it for a moment. Of course, it's all Attlee's and Bevan's fault. They're both asses, if you'll pardon my saying so."

"His Majesty's government has to be evenhanded in its treatment of the Jews and the Arabs of this country," said the major, as if reading from a speech.

Melanie dismissed his remark with a wave of her hand.

He continued, "You can always remain in Cyprus and try the representatives of the Jewish Agency there. They live in the Hotel Savoy in Famagusta and will no doubt find a way to get you into the detention camp, which is more than I, as a British officer, am capable of. There have been riots and acts of violence there, and we're anxious to prevent more."

"How long do you think my nephew will have to stay there?"

"Judging by the number of illegal immigrants now in detention, it will be many months before he can get a visa under the quota."

"How big is the quota?"

"One thousand five hundred Jews are allowed into Palestine every month."

"Is there any chance of his jumping to the head of the line?"

"No. We and the Jewish Agency are both very careful not to do that. I can remember at least one case in which an agency representative tried to move up a family relation and was recalled at once."

"Then you'll have to help me get my nephew out of there. I made Theresa a promise, and I intend to keep it."

"Even if it costs me my commission?" joked the major.

"Major Scott," said Melanie, a note of determination creeping into her voice, "I'm not going to Cyprus without bringing him back from there. I'm getting tired of all these wild goose chases. It's time for results, and I mean to obtain them, even if I have to smuggle him out in a suitcase. Everyone knows that a rich English lady traveling in the Middle East requires some very large pieces of luggage."

"Lady Faulkner, I won't desert you now. As long as I'm not risking my neck or betraying my country, I'm at your service." He smiled. "I'm happy to see you show a fighting spirit."

They shook hands like two partisans who have just concluded a secret pact.

No sooner had Melanie returned to her hotel than Major Scott was on the phone. "What's happened?" she asked.

"There's a dispute between the British authorities in Cyprus and those here," he told her. "Those in Cyprus don't want any more Palestinians without papers, and those here don't want any more illegal immigrants. The fact of the matter is that I don't believe the real problem is the papers. They don't want the Palestinians in Cyprus because they stir up too much trouble in the camps."

"Where is the ship bound for, then?"

"Along the coast."

"But why didn't it just stay in port?"

"Because we were afraid of disturbances. In any event, I'll keep you posted."

"Thank you, Major Scott," said Melanie. "I'm most grateful."

She lay down for a nap and slept until evening. Major Scott did not call again, and when Melanie woke she heard on the radio that seven hundred stateless Jews had been deported to Cyprus aboard the *Empire Royal*. She telephoned James and brought him up-to-date.

"But why," he asked, "don't you just sit tight in Jerusalem until the immigrants are put somewhere permanent, either in Cyprus or elsewhere, and then . . . ?"

"You don't understand," Melanie told him. "Until now I've been looking for him for my sake, and it's enough for me to know that he exists even if I can't see him or let him know that I exist. But now I have to reunite him with Theresa."

"You know, Melanie, for some time now I've been thinking that this whole expedition of yours is not just because of —"

She didn't let him finish. She knew what he was going to say.

"That's exactly what Henya, my friend on the kibbutz, thinks too."

There was a long silence at the other end of the line.
"James, are you there?"
"Yes," said James. "Where should I be?"
"I love you," said Melanie.

15.
Yulek Helps Himself

It was a hard night for everyone. At dawn the first
returnees from the deck reported that the coast of Cyprus was in sight. Vats of sweetened tea with milk tasting of powder were lowered to them, and Yulek drank
some of it. The sea was calmer and he felt better. The
bulkhead resounded with a steady drumbeat as the
leaders of the two compartments made joint plans
for resisting disembarkation. Yulek roused himself and
joined a group of youngsters in making preparations.

Their main worry was that the soldiers would force
them to leave the ship by lobbing tear gas canisters or
smoke grenades into the hold. Their instructions were
to cover these immediately with wet blankets and toss
the bundles into the hold below them, and they were
told to collect as much water as they could in the containers that had held their K rations. And so, before the
bemused eyes of the soldiers guarding the deck, Yulek
and the others kept going for more water. They also
found a long, heavy metal rod, which they planned to

use as a battering ram to break down the walls of the compartment in case they needed air.

Two hours passed before the ship lowered its anchor and came to a halt, rocking gently outside Famagusta Harbor. The "bathroom lookout" informed them that the harbor looked too small for their ship and that most likely they would be taken ashore in launches. Indeed, a new group of observers soon came back with the news that landing craft were approaching the ship.

An officer stuck his head through the vent and ordered them to start coming up. Greeted by a chorus of jeers, he replied with a threat to use force. Six helmeted soldiers with clubs descended the ladder and began forcing the hold's occupants to climb out. Someone flung his mess kit at them, and in no time the air was filled with dozens of projectiles. The soldiers hurriedly retreated up the ladder, some leaving behind their helmets and clubs.

The officer returned and announced that he would be compelled to use tear gas if the deportees did not leave the ship voluntarily. No one made a move to comply. A number of tear gas canisters were lobbed down at them, after which the vent was sealed with wooden planks to keep the smoke from escaping. Yulek and his team swung into action, wrapping the canisters in wet blankets and tossing them into the hold below. Meanwhile a group of musclemen pounded at the bulkhead with the battering ram, backing off and charging at it again and again. Before long it caved in, and the fresh air helped dilute the gas.

Not enough, though. By now some of the deportees,

especially the older ones, were beginning to choke and feel sick, and soon they decided to abandon the struggle. The British opened the vent, and the deportees began to ascend the ladders, with those suffering the most from the smoke going first. Coughing and blood-shot, Yulek came on deck and breathed deeply.

A tall man with a large mustache, who introduced himself as the Jewish Agency's Cyprus representative, was waiting for them on deck. The Palestinians knew him by name. As soon as he told them that the decision had been made at the highest level to offer no further resistance, they descended into the launches in perfect order and reached shore within a few minutes. Although a number of ambulances with open doors were waiting there, no one was hurt badly enough to need them, and the entire shipload of deportees was loaded quietly onto trucks and driven to a detention camp.

Once again they were behind barbed wire. The camp was a small quarantine station in which, they were told, they would be held for several days before being trans-ferred to more permanent quarters. Two armored cars carrying machine guns were posted at the gate.

This time the British soldiers and the group's Pales-tinian leaders worked together. Everyone stood in line to receive a mess tin and blankets and then went to a tent that had mattresses and army cots. Next a pickup truck with a Greek driver arrived with vats of hot food. Yulek volunteered to help dish out the food. There were potatoes, soup, sliced bread, and an unidentifiable glop, and whoever was hungry enough ate his fill.

Yulek moved into a tent with Rivka, Bella, Frieda,

and a few other old friends from the villa in Italy. After they had eaten and arranged their things, they stretched out on the cots to rest.

Yulek had barely shut his eyes when a Palestinian walked in and said, "My name is Gabi, and I come from a kibbutz called Givat Brenner. We've just been told that we'll be here for two days, at the end of which there will be one last selection. We've decided to put one of us in each tent so we can prep you on a particular kibbutz to help you pass."

Then I have one more chance, thought Yulek, picturing the smile on Theresa's face when she would see him. This time he would be a good student and pass the test. *Just a few more days, Theresa,* he vowed.

"Does that mean that the kibbutz you tell us about is the one we'll be sent to?" he asked Gabi.

"That's correct" was the answer.

"Then I want to change tents," Yulek said, starting to gather his things.

Rivka watched him with big, mournful eyes.

"Yulek, don't be an idiot," said Frieda, realizing his motive at once.

Yulek finished repacking, said goodbye, and left the tent. Rivka ran after him.

"I'm sorry, Rivka," he said. "It's because of Theresa."

"You don't honestly think we'll keep teasing her about that silly cross, do you?"

"No, especially not if she gets over it herself. But you know . . . even though I like you very much . . ."

Rivka began to cry. She cried quietly, with no change of expression, the tears running down her cheeks. Yulek hugged her, but when she clung to him with all her might he realized that it had been the wrong thing to do. He made himself let go of her, picked up his things, and walked off without hearing whatever it was she called after him. Striding off quickly to the other end of the camp, he found a tent with an empty cot and put his things down on it.

"Is it all right if I move in here?" he asked the tent's occupants.

They belonged to the group with which Theresa had come to the villa, and although he did not remember any of them, most of them knew him. While Yulek was making his cot, a Palestinian entered and repeated the speech he had heard before. The man's name was Yankele, and he had come from a kibbutz called Shibolet. He was older than most of the other Palestinians, perhaps even older than his frank suntanned face made him look.

Yankele's main request was that everyone in the tent change his first name to a Hebrew one. This took a while, because not everyone was happy with the names suggested. One girl said that she did not want a new name. Yankele didn't argue. He simply told her that this would make it harder for her to pass the selection.

"All right, I'll do it," she said. "But only for the selection."

Since the Hebrew name Yuval sounded a bit like Yulek and the Hebrew word for gold was *zahav,* Yulek Goldenberg became Yuval Zahavi. "Terrific," said Yankele, turning to the next one in line.

Yulek's new name felt very strange.

When they were done renaming themselves, they began their lessons. These lasted two and a half days, with short recesses for meals and other necessities. Yankele woke them early in the morning and kept them up until late at night while they memorized all the details of their supposed home in Palestine. Little by little they came to know Shibolet so well that one might have thought they really lived there.

"Do you mean to tell us that the English actually know all these things themselves?" asked someone incredulously

"No. But they'll have with them a Jewish police officer who does his homework just like us. And the British secret police are very knowledgeable too."

Yulek made a supreme effort to remember everything: the names of his fellow kibbutzniks, what bus he had to take to Shibolet from Tel Aviv, how often it left, how much a ticket cost, what color it was, and in what direction the sea lay as the bus traveled. He even remembered that an ice cream cone cost half a piaster and a strip of apricot leather one Palestinian mil.

"What's apricot leather?" he wanted to know.

"It's apricot jam dried in thin squares in the sun until it becomes tough and leathery," explained Yankele, whose patience appeared to be inexhaustible.

Yulek memorized the annual winter rainfall in Shibolet (in summer it didn't rain at all), and how long it took to walk to the nearest settlements. He learned how the kibbutz elected its leaders, how a general assembly took place, who was responsible for the security patrols, and who guarded Shibolet's fields.

"Hayyim, our field guard, is very tall, a good head taller than I am," Yankele told them. "That's why we call him Hayyim-and-a-Half."

Yuval Zahavi learned how many cows were in Shibolet's barn and how many chickens in its coops. He learned all about its furniture factory and its foundry.

"It's your factory and your foundry," said Yankele. "It's your kibbutz."

Yulek learned that Shibolet had one hundred fifty adult members and forty children. He learned that breakfast was bread, a fresh vegetable, a dab of jam and margarine, tea, and half an egg (*Half an egg?* Yankele assured him that he had heard right); that lunch was soup, cereal, meatballs, a boiled vegetable, and sometimes stewed fruit; and that supper was the same as breakfast with an extra wedge of cheese. He also learned that there was another Zahavi, who was the kibbutz landscaper.

"But I don't have to tell *you* that — he's your uncle," said Yankele, and everyone laughed.

For some reason Yulek suddenly thought of Rivka and felt badly. *I had to do it,* he told himself, *not only for Theresa, but for Rivka's sake too.* He was aware that deep down he still enjoyed knowing that she was desperately in love with him and that it had been selfish of him not to make things clear to her long ago. Well, at least he had done so now. He was still thinking about it when a question of Yankele's recalled him to his studies.

It rained the night before the fateful day, but the sky was blue when they stepped outside for breakfast in the freshly washed morning. Yulek had a good feeling. He was sure he would pass the test. After breakfast was dished out, the British soldiers set up three long tables, and the detainees were told to assemble with their mess tins and blankets. According to Yankele, five of the chairs were for British secret service agents and the sixth was for the Jewish policeman. At the last minute two more chairs were added. These were occupied by a British officer and lady who had arrived in a small military vehicle. The lady was middle-aged and wore a large purple hat.

"Do you see that woman?" Yankele whispered to Yulek. "I've seen her before, at the British army camp we were first held at. It was the evening we were put on the buses," he continued, trying to be exact. "I was sitting in the parade grounds and looking at a shack opposite me. Suddenly one of the shack's windows opened, and she stuck her head out and shouted, 'Yulek! Yulek!' She was even wearing the same hat. I swear she's the one!"

"Yulek?" Yulek was startled.

"Yes. Why?"

"That's my name."

"She shouted a family name too," said Yankele, trying to remember. "Wait, don't tell me. It was something like Goldman or Goldberg — a name like that."

"My name is Yulek Goldenberg!"

"You don't happen to have a cousin in Palestine who's on intimate terms with the English, do you?" asked Yankele.

"No," Yulek said. "But I do have an aunt in England."

"Maybe she's come to look for you."

"She has no way of knowing that I'm here, or even that I'm alive. She lives in London, and all I know is her first name. I once knew her family name too, but I've forgotten it."

"Why, it must be that friend of Henya's!" Yankele exclaimed, clapping Yulek on the shoulder.

He told Yulek about Lady Melanie Faulkner, who was planning to come to the kibbutz to visit her old school friend from Warsaw.

"She was supposed to arrive the night your ship did," said Yankele. "I'll bet it's the same woman."

He had to grab Yulek hard to keep the boy from running to the Englishwoman. "Tell her who you are, and you'll be stuck here a long time," he said.

Yulek stopped short, his head in a whirl. He strained to get a glimpse of the woman, but she was sitting too far away and her hat hid her face. He knew that his aunt had looked for him in Poland and probably checked the available records there, but how could she have known he was here? And yet Christian or not, here she was! It made no sense at all.

"I can't believe it," he said.

"Well," repeated Yankele, "she did shout Yulek Gold-something. I'm sure of it. But keep calm, that's the main thing, or else you'll fail the selection. You can always look for her again later. Or she'll find a way to locate you. I just hope she doesn't realize who you are now."

"But how will I find Theresa?"

"It's a small country, and she'll probably be in a kibbutz near Shibolet. Look, Yuval, if you want to pass the selection, listen to me and forget all that. Forget even what you've learned from me. You have to have a clear head. You have to feel that you know everything and have perfect confidence. You can say the dumbest things to your interrogator, but if you sound like you believe them, so will he. After all, for you he's special, but for him you're just one of a long line of faces. He may be tired or in a hurry to get to the end of the line. And even if you don't make it, you can always turn to your aunt then. But I'm sure you'll convince them that you're Yuval Zahavi. You're already as suntanned as a Palestinian."

"I suppose it's from the ship," said Yulek distractedly, glancing at the lady in the hat.

Yankele grinned at him. "If you pull it off, I promise to help you find her. The more I think of it, the surer I am that she's my wife's old friend. That means you have nothing to worry about. Just keep your mind on what matters."

"Will you be going back now too?"

"Yes. I'm too old for a long stay here. I have permission to tell the British who I am. When did your aunt last see you?"

"When I was seven or eight."

"Then you're lucky. She'll never be able to identify you."

But suppose she did and he was left in Cyprus? Yulek couldn't stop worrying. He decided that nothing would make him admit that he was Malka's nephew. And yet he was afraid of losing her. For the first time since the end of the war, he had found someone from his family: someone who had known his parents, the house he grew up in, his brothers and sisters; someone who remembered his childhood and all the other lost things that now existed only in his memory, as if they were something he had imagined. All it took was one other person to remember them too — to throw his memories a lifeline — and they would become real again. If she truly was his aunt, who had managed in some mysterious manner to locate him, how could he risk letting her vanish again?

Melanie was worried too. After all the young faces she had seen in the past few days, her faith in her ability to identify her nephew was shaken. She looked again at his photographs and those of her brother. Clearly she had been able to recognize Yulek in the newspaper because they both had the same peculiar expression that comes from facing a photographer. Suppose Yulek didn't have it now? And Major Scott had kept reminding her that she must pretend not to know him if she didn't want the British to hold him in Cyprus. Afterward, he had said, he himself or the Jewish Agency would be able to put them in touch again.

All Melanie really wanted was to see her nephew. At least once.

"Can't you use your influence to get him into Palestine?" she had asked the major.

"No."

"But you used it to get me into the interrogation."

"Right. But the interrogators will want to make a

good impression on me by doing their work thoroughly. They've already asked me for the name of the boy you're looking for."

"What did you tell them?"

"Edmond Friede."

"Why Edmond Friede?"

"That was the name of a friend of mine when I studied at Oxford. He was a Polish Jew too."

"Do you think my nephew will give them his real name?"

"Maybe his family name. Many of them take a Hebrew first name but don't change their last one."

Melanie had tried to imagine what would happen. "If I'm spotted there by some Jewish Agency official, they'll never talk to me again," she had said.

"All you'll have to do then, Lady Faulkner, is move to another hotel, change your clothes, and above all take off that hat of yours, and no one will know who you are. Although I'm sure that even then, your beauty will make you conspicuous."

"Thank you," Melanie had said in a surprised voice. Until then, Major Scott had seemed too much the British gentleman to say such a thing to a woman, especially to one who was thirty-seven years old.

The major had driven her to the detention camp, and the selection had started on schedule. The hundreds of detainees stood sitting or standing at a distance from the tables. The interrogators apologized for sitting with their backs to her. It took a good deal of reassuring to convince them that she wasn't offended.

There were six of them, one a police officer who

Major Scott said was a Jew. A sergeant gave an order, and the detainees formed a line, each stepping up in turn to the first available interrogator. To their surprise, the British plainclothes men spoke a rudimentary Hebrew that was, as Major Scott explained to Melanie, quite sufficient for the questions they had to ask. Although she did not understand a word of it, Melanie quickly realized that the first two questions put to everyone were about his or her name and address. As soon as each interrogation was finished, the sergeant called out, "Next!"

It went on and on.

Most of those questioned were turned back. Yet quite a few were released and shown to an exit, where they were instructed to throw their blankets and mess tins into a truck and climb onto a second truck, which slowly began to fill up.

"Where will they be taken?" asked Melanie.

"Back to the port, Lady Faulkner," replied the major.

It struck her that he made a point of calling her Lady Faulkner in the presence of the British interrogators.

"Next!"

On and on.

And then all at once there he was. Melanie recognized him immediately. He could have been her brother come back to life and approaching her with the long, measured steps she knew so well. "That's Yulek!" she whispered in Major Scott's ear. "I'm sure of it."

Although the major had to lay a hand on her shoulder to keep her from leaping up, she quickly regained her self-possession and showed no excitement apart from her eyes, which stayed glued to Yulek. He gave his interrogator an unfamiliar Hebrew name. His next answer — "Shibolet" — was a word she knew.

Yulek found himself facing the Jewish police officer. He wasn't worried about his Hebrew, which was good enough. Nor did he look at the woman with the hat who was sitting behind the interrogators. He was afraid that even one glance at her would make him lose his concentration.

"Name?"

"Yuval Zahavi."

"Where do you live?"

"Kibbutz Shibolet."

"Where do you work?"

"In the flower nursery."

"Who's in charge of it?"

"Sachs."

"How long does it take to walk in Tel Aviv from one end of Allenby Street to the other?"

"I have no idea. It's not an area I've ever walked in."

"What's the name of the mayor of Haifa?"

"Beats me."

"How much does a bus ticket from Shibolet to Tel Aviv cost?"

"A piaster and a half."

"What color is the ticket?"

"Green."

"Do you know Hayyim?"

Yulek's heart skipped a beat. *This is my chance,* he thought. He looked the interrogator straight in the face and asked, "You aren't by any chance thinking of Hayyim-and-a-Half, are you?"

"Go throw your things in the first truck and get on the second."

Yulek could have jumped in the air for sheer joy. Then he remembered the lady in the hat. He turned to look at her and saw his aunt. A dim childhood memory of someone young and beautiful came back to him, and he saw his aunt Malka standing in the yard of their old house, feeding the chickens — the same Aunt Malka whose photograph he had discovered in his mother's book. He was, he knew, taking too much time, but he couldn't stop looking at her.

Without warning she asked him in Yiddish, "Young man, what was your father's name?"

"Artur," he answered without thinking. Then, alarmed, he moved away from the table without looking back.

The two plainclothes men sitting in front of Melanie turned around and asked, "Is that the lad you're looking for?"

"No," said Melanie, trying to keep her voice steady. "I'm afraid not."

She no longer had any reason to stay, and after a while she asked the major in a whisper if they could leave. He shook his head.

"You'll have to sit through this to the end. There's nothing to do about it."

The truck of released detainees was almost full. Yulek stood in a corner, glancing now and then at his aunt. He had no doubt that it was Malka. He was no longer alone in the world! Of course, he wasn't alone anyway as long as he had Theresa, but this put an end to a different kind of loneliness. It was the loneliness of a small child left all by himself, and which one of us hasn't felt it sometimes?

He watched Rivka fail the test and get sent back. Bella passed. Frieda didn't. An argument broke out. Apparently they were telling the British that they were sisters. The interrogator sent both of them back. Yulek felt sorry for them, though not as sorry as he did for Rivka. Perhaps he should have stayed in the tent with her. No one, after all, could have forced him to live in Givat Brenner if Theresa had wanted to be somewhere else.

The truck set out, and he and Melanie exchanged parting glances. A new truck drove up to take its place. From time to time the interrogators stopped for a coffee break, and at noon they adjourned for lunch. The hours crawled as slowly as the soft March sun that crossed the sky overhead and started to sink. The last detainee was questioned. The interrogators rose, and some soldiers folded the tables.

Just then, as if responding to a signal, dozens of men rushed forward and insisted that they were Palestinians. The interrogators debated what to do, but the protesters' self-confidence persuaded them to reopen the proceedings.

This time everything went quickly. The new group, which had not come forward until now, spoke a native Hebrew, knew all the right answers, showed no sign of hesitation in giving them, and looked their questioners straight in the eye. In less than an hour they had joined the convoy to the port.

Melanie and Major Scott got into their car and drove behind the trucks for a while. Although the road was narrow, they passed them and reached the port first. This time there was no barbed wire or armed troops. Melanie stood with the major on the pier, in vain looking for Yulek in the throng by the ship's railing. The boarding ramp was lifted. The anchor was raised. And still she stood rooted to the spot.

"I know it's not important," she said to Major Scott, "but I feel such a need to talk with him, even if to say only one word. Now!"

The engines throbbed, and the propeller churned up the water at the stern. With a blast of its horn the ship began to leave its berth. Just then Melanie caught sight of a slim, lanky young man. She took off her hat and waved it as hard as she could.

"It's I!" shouted Yulek.

"Yulek!" shouted Melanie.

"Aunt Malka!" he shouted, waving back. "Aunt Malka!"

That did it. She broke into tears and cried and cried without trying to stop. The crowd on deck was singing "Hatikvah." Melanie joined in even though she didn't know the words.

16.
Five Letters

May 15, 1947
Kibbutz Shibolet

Dear Mela,

I was very happy to get your letter. Everything is fine with us. Yankele is in charge of a group of new immigrants and is enjoying Yuval-Yulek and Theresa immensely. (Theresa has been adamant about keeping her Polish name.)

Udi, our baby son, is growing up fast. We're thrilled with him. To tell you the truth — I've even quarreled about this with Yankele — I can't stand putting him to bed in the children's house at night and leaving him there until morning. I know he cries for me when he's hungry and wants to nurse, and I'm sure that the housemother doesn't always call for me when that happens. Sometimes she's too lazy and makes do with giving him a bit of sugar water, and sometimes it's for the ridiculous principle of the thing: if nursing mothers are woken at night, they won't have the strength to work the next day. I've already been called before the Social Committee for leaving him with us in our room at night and letting him sleep in our bed. That makes them furious, because, they say, it sets a bad precedent for all the young couples. For the first time I'm beginning to wonder if this is a place I want to go on living in. Yankele and I have even discussed leaving. You should know that since Udi was born, Yankele too is no longer the ardent kibbutznik he used to be. There's a difference between being a father and being an old bachelor, and many things that didn't bother him before now do.

Well, I won't bore you with any more of this. The situation in the country is very tense. The roads are dangerous to travel, and I'm afraid that if the British pull out one day, we'll have a full-scale war with the Arabs. There are six hundred thousand of us, and you only need look at a map to see how many Arabs there are. But Yankele is optimistic. He says that history shows that a people that fights for its freedom succeeds in getting it in the end. I hope he's right and that we'll be able to hold our own. He has such confidence in our leaders and in the commanders of the underground organizations. What can I tell you? A man of faith! I'm so lucky to have found such a loving and devoted husband at my age.

Yulek and Theresa will write to you separately. I send you my love, and warmest regards from Yankele. When will we see you again?

Yours,
Henya

P.S. I've just read today's newspaper and am terribly excited. Perhaps Yankele is right to be so hopeful. I'm talking about the speech given at the UN by the

Russian ambassador Gromyko in which he came out in support of a Jewish state. And it really is time that we had one, after all our suffering and wandering for two thousand years.

June 2, 1947

Dear Melanie,

I'm in a training group, living in the same tent you saw me in when you were here. We are working very hard and studying a bit of Hebrew and half a day a week of other subjects. All day long I wait for Yulek to come back in the evening from work. Everyone here except me calls him Yuval. I'm always worried about him because he's the security guard on a bus. There's an Arab village near here called Akir, and now and then shots are fired from it at Jewish buses. But it does make me proud to see Yulek with his rifle and military cap.

I have many new friends here, and at night we lie on the lawn near the dining room and sing. Afterward Yulek and I go for walks in the fields, and sometimes there's a big Palestinian moon shining down on us. I love Yulek so much. When I'm eighteen — and that's only two years away — we'll get married if he still loves me the way he does now. Do you think you could come to our wedding? Kibbutz weddings are very nice. We had one here not long ago. How could we get married without you? I think about you all the time. And oh, yes, I almost forgot: you have warm regards from Robert. He comes to visit now and then and brings all kinds of goodies. He bought himself a camera, and we all had our pictures taken. He brought a few of them for you the last time he was here, and I'm sending them with this letter. Yulek wants to add a few words.

With much, much love,
Theresa

Dear Melanie,

We're all fine. Theresa says that she wrote to you about my job. You don't have to worry about it. It's not so dangerous, and I enjoy getting to Tel Aviv now and then. When Theresa gets a day off she comes with me, and if there's enough time between trips, we go for a stroll along Allenby Street. At the selection in Cyprus I was asked how long it takes to walk it. Now I know! We stop for an ice cream and a soda and sometimes take a dip in the sea. It's too bad that Theresa gets so few days off.

She didn't want to show me her letter to you, because she said it was private. I can imagine what she must have written! I can only add that I love her very much. She's the most beautiful girl I've ever seen. Don't you agree?

I hope we'll work out our problems with the English and the Arabs and soon have a state of our own. Maybe one day we'll even visit you in London. We're

sending you two photographs, one of me and Theresa
and one of the two of us with Robert. They were
both taken with his camera. He sends you regards.
He's still in Tel Aviv and involved in all kinds of business — exactly what, he never says.

I loved getting the copies of the photographs that
you sent me. I really do look a lot like my father.
And I was very happy to get a copy of the family por-
trait too. My mother looks sad in it. Why do you
think that is? My father looks very solemn, and all the
children are funny and sweet — just how I remember
them.

I can't tell you how much I hate the Germans.
Sometimes I think that if I could get hold of an atom
bomb and drop it on Berlin, I would do it. But then I
think of all the innocent people, the mothers and the
children, and I'm not so sure that I could go through
with it. There are people there who feel and love and
laugh and cry and believe just like me. How could I
kill them all? And how could they have killed us? It's
too much for me to understand.

On the subject of believing, I'm sure Theresa didn't
mention something. When we visited Jerusalem with
some kibbutzniks, we stepped into an important
church there, a really famous one, and suddenly Theresa disappeared. I'm sure she went off to some corner to pray. I don't blame her, either. Not everyone
has the ability to pray, and I envy those who do.
Maybe it's something you have to be brought up with.
If you were raised to pray in a synagogue, that's the

only place where you'll ever be able to do it, and the same holds true for a church. Only there can you open your heart to what people call God. Do you believe in Him? I do. Not in a God who's like a father or a grandfather with a long beard. But I do believe that there's something beyond us that we can never understand. Something that's beyond all imagination or logic, even all science. But I don't know what that something wants of us, and there's really no point in trying to guess.

Theresa is proud of me. I told her I was going to add two more lines, and here I've written a whole letter! Well, this is where I stop.

With love forever,
Yulek

Monday, August 4, 1947
Haifa Port

Dear Theresa and Yulek,

This is a farewell letter. When you get it I'll be far out at sea, on my way to America, the Land of Opportunity. I can already see you shaking your heads pityingly at me for being a miserable slave of Mammon and the golden calf. It's easy for two people in love to criticize someone who isn't — at least yet. Meanwhile . . .

During my short stay on the kibbutz I came to realize one thing: life there wasn't for me. Nor is Tel Aviv the place I want to start out in. I'll tell you something else: the kibbutz isn't for Theresa either. And maybe not even for you, Yulek. You'll get along in it, though. Theresa will suffer.

I won't deny that I feel guilty about leaving this country. It's my country too, and it needs every Jew it can get. Let's face it: I'm an egoist. That's something I learned during the six years of the war. I'm the only one in my family to have survived, and I intend to get rich, marry, and have lots of children, who will never have to worry about money.

The decision wasn't an easy one. Even after I found people to pull the right strings for me, I wasn't sure if I really would go. But now my mind is made up.

I'm at the port, in Haifa, in the passengers' waiting room. I'm about to travel the same route we did half a year ago, but in the opposite direction. I'm sailing to France on the *Champollion,* and from there I'll make my way to America.

I send you hugs and kisses with this letter. I should have come to say goodbye in person, but it would have been too painful for me. Perhaps for you too. Be well, Yulek and Theresa.

Yours,
Robert

September 21, 1947

Dearest Henya,

I'm pregnant! I kept it a secret for the first three months. But the doctor says that everything is fine. We're thrilled!

I was very happy to hear of the recommendation by the United Nations Special Committee on Palestine to establish a Jewish state. James thinks that the UN General Assembly will vote for the plan over British objections, because the Americans and Russians will back it despite the hostility between them. You can count on James to know such things. There will be a Jewish state and an Arab one, with Jerusalem an international city. And with that the British Mandate will come to an end. It makes me both worried and glad.

Kisses to all of you,
Melanie

Uri Orlev, himself a Holocaust survivor, is the author of four books based on his and others' actual experiences during and after World War II: *The Island on Bird Street* (winner of the Mildred L. Batchelder Award, Sydney Taylor Book Award, Janusz Korczak Literary Prize), *The Man from the Other Side* (winner of the Mildred L. Batchelder Award, National Jewish Book Award), *Lydia, Queen of Palestine*, and *The Lady with the Hat* (winner of the Mildred L. Batchelder Award).

In 1996 he received the prestigious Hans Christian Andersen Award for the body of his work.